## "So family is important to you now," Zoey said without thinking.

She hadn't meant to add to his pain, but she had lived through her son's silent suffering, through the years of watching Dane go off on one assignment after another, leaving her and the children alone to cope with his prolonged absences.

Dane flinched. "Ouch. You're certainly blunt."

"Something I've learned to be over the past few years. A lot about me has changed."

"And a lot about me has changed."

"Then we aren't the same two people who married fourteen years ago?" she asked.

"No, and being strangers isn't a good foundation for a marriage."

"I agree. But we have three children and we made a vow before God that I intend to keep."

**THE LADIES OF SWEETWATER LAKE:**
**Like a wedding ring, this circle of friends**
**is never ending.**

## Books by Margaret Daley

Love Inspired

*The Power of Love* #168
*Family for Keeps* #183
*Sadie's Hero* #191
*The Courage To Dream* #205
*What the Heart Knows* #236
*A Family for Tory* #245
*\*Gold in the Fire* #273
*\*A Mother for Cindy* #283
*\*Light in the Storm* #297
*The Cinderella Plan* #320
*\*When Dreams Come True* #339

*The Ladies of Sweetwater Lake

## MARGARET DALEY

feels she has been blessed. She has been married more than thirty years to her husband, Mike, whom she met in college. He is a terrific support and her best friend. They have one son, Shaun.

Margaret has been writing for many years and loves to tell a story. When she was a little girl, she would play with her dolls and make up stories about their lives. Now she writes these stories down. She especially enjoys weaving stories about families and how faith in God can sustain a person when things get tough. When she isn't writing, she is fortunate to be a teacher for students with special needs. Margaret has taught for over twenty years and loves working with her students. She has also been a Special Olympics coach and participated in many sports with her students.

# WHEN DREAMS
# COME TRUE
# MARGARET DALEY

Steeple
Hill®

Published by Steeple Hill Books™

STEEPLE HILL BOOKS

ISBN 0-373-81253-1

WHEN DREAMS COME TRUE

Copyright © 2006 by Margaret Daley

www.SteepleHill.com

Printed in U.S.A.

Be merciful to me, O God, be merciful to me!
For my soul trusts in You; and in the shadow of
Your wings I will make my refuge, until these
calamities have passed by.

—*Psalms* 57:1

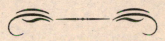

To my husband, Mike, who is a wonderful support, and to my son, Shaun, whom I am blessed to have as a son. I love you both.

# Chapter One

"**M**ommy! There's a man here to see ya!" Mandy Witherspoon yelled.

With a shake of her head, Zoey Witherspoon dried her hands on a towel. "Mom, I don't know how many times I've told that child never to open the door to a stranger. Will she ever learn to listen?"

Emma Bradford laughed. "You should have seen you at that age. You want me to see who it is?"

"No, I will, then have a word with my daughter. It's a good thing we live in a safe, small town." Already headed toward the kitchen door, Zoey glanced at the clock over the desk and realized how late the hour was. Who would be visiting right before the children's bedtime?

When Zoey stepped into the foyer and saw a tall, thin man through the screen, she held back the scream that demanded release. She blinked. Her eyes had to be playing tricks on her. But when she focused on the man again, she realized the impossible had occurred.

The pounding of her heart threatened to squeeze the air from her lungs. Slowly she moved toward the front door, past her daughter. "Mandy, go help your grandmother clean up."

The sound of her daughter racing toward the kitchen faded, and all Zoey heard was the thundering beat of her heart pulsating in her ears. She opened the screen door to get a better look at the man on her front porch.

Her eyes slid closed. *It can't be Dane.*

Zoey braced herself with a deep, fortifying breath and opened her eyes to stare at the man who had returned from the dead. She took the few steps separating them and laid her hand on his chest to feel the strong beat of his heart against her palm, to assess what she was seeing was real—very real. Then without a word, she threw herself into his embrace.

He kissed the top of her head, then her forehead and finally her lips. A brief, searing touch of their mouths that left Zoey even more shaken. The warmth of his body emphasized how alive her husband was.

Finally pulling away and looking up into the face that had haunted her dreams for the past two-and-a-half years, she whispered her husband's name, "Dane."

"Hello, Zoey."

"They told me you were dead. I—" No other words came to mind. Releasing the doorknob that she'd clutched so tightly to keep herself upright, she stepped back to allow him into the house.

"They were wrong." One corner of his mouth lifted in a self-mocking grin that didn't stay long.

Tears welled into her eyes at the sight of him. He was thin, almost gaunt. His face was clean shaven, but she could tell that he'd worn a beard until recently. His black hair was cut short and sprinkled with strands of gray now, even though he was only thirty-eight. Before he had left on his last assignment he had never had any gray. But the most startling difference in her husband was his eyes. When she looked into them, she saw nothing of the man she'd known and loved. For a brief moment she'd glimpsed a vulnerability in his eyes that he would never have allowed to show in the past. A shiver flashed down her spine as she realized he was a stranger to her.

Standing in the middle of her foyer in her home in Sweetwater, she swallowed several times, feeling as lost as he had been to her. "What happened, Dane?" she asked, her words thick with the tears she was frantic to keep bottled inside. She'd fallen apart once before—when she'd heard the news of his death. It had taken so long to claw her way out of the emotional abyss she'd wallowed in. She vowed then she would never put herself in that position again. She had more than herself to think about.

"As you know, the plane crashed over the Amazon. I was lucky. I was thrown from the plane when it hit the trees. The Xinga tribe saw the fire from the crash, found me unconscious and nursed me back to health." A shutter dropped over his features. "I didn't know who I was until recently."

The thought of what he must have gone through threatened to overwhelm her. She again touched his arm, weaved her fingers through his as though that link would solidify her dream of her husband returning to her and the children. He still stood in the foyer. This was no vision, but reality. "You had amnesia?"

Dane sidestepped away from her touch and turned into the living room. He sought a chair and sat as though he physically couldn't stand any longer. "Yes. For a long time I only had glimpses of my life, but nothing to help me piece together who I was."

"How about the other two people in the plane?" She sat across from him, her own weariness after a long day at work catching up with her.

"From what the Xingas told me, because I was thrown from the plane, I was saved. The pilot and Bob Patterson weren't. There was little left of the plane, only bits and pieces that had broken off from the main body before it caught on fire." He released a heavy sigh. "I know you have a lot of questions, but I'd rather not go into the details right now."

"But, Dane—"

"Please," he cut in, his blue eyes continuing to convey that vulnerability she never would have associated with her husband. "I realize when I left we were talking about separating, but I hope I can stay here for a while. I need..." His voice trailed off into silence.

"Of course," she said to fill the awkwardness that had descended. There would be time later to discuss what had happened between them right before he'd gone on his last assignment, to talk about what he had gone through the past two-and-a-half years. "Blake has grown a lot. He's going to be tall like you. In fact, he's the spitting image of you."

"Oh, that's too bad," Dane said with a lopsided grin that she'd often thought of as cocky, but not now.

"And Mandy will be so excited when she realizes that it was you in the foyer." Zoey paused to catch her breath. "She just didn't recognize you. She was so young when you... disappeared."

A soft expression entered his eyes. "She looks like you. She's beautiful."

Zoey peered away. There was so much she needed to tell him, so much she needed to understand. "There's something else."

He straightened, one brow arching.

"We have another daughter, Tara. She was born seven months after you—" Zoey paused for a few seconds, having almost said *died* "—left."

"Another daughter?"

The wonder in his voice tore at Zoey's defenses. Tears burned her eyes. She'd shed so many that first year Dane had been gone. How could there possibly be any left?

"Yes, that's one of the reasons I came back to Sweetwater." *And the fact I hated living in*

*Dallas, lost in the crowd of people with no family there as support.* She remembered the struggle to pull herself together after Dane had disappeared. For years her life had revolved around him until she wasn't even sure there had been a Zoey Witherspoon, a person independent from her husband. She didn't want to get tangled up in that kind of pain ever again.

"So much has changed. I can't believe I have three…." Silence snatched the rest of his sentence.

Zoey waited for Dane to continue. She needed him to tell her more, to share with her what he was feeling, thinking. He surged to his feet and began to pace as though he were an animal confined to a small cage and checking out his domain.

That was the Dane she was used to—the man who shut her out of his life, who kept secrets from her because of his job in the DEA, who was driven by a restless energy. *Please, Heavenly Father, help me to be strong.*

Zoey leaned forward, resting her elbows on her knees and clasping her hands together. "Does your boss know you're alive?"

"Yes."

Shocked by his answer, Zoey asked in a voice laden with budding anger, "Why didn't Carl let me know you were?"

"I told him not to. I wanted to be the one to tell you face to face. I didn't think it was something that should be handled over the phone or by a stranger appearing at your door. Too impersonal."

"What are your plans, Dane?"

He stopped his pacing, tension coming off him in waves. "Would you believe I don't have any plans at the moment?"

That was hard to believe because her husband had always been so focused. "How about your job at the DEA?"

He raked his hand through his short hair. "I don't know. Carl told me to take some time off and we'd talk when I've fully recovered. He encouraged me to get reacquainted with my family."

That surprised Zoey. In the past his boss had always demanded one hundred percent from Dane. To Carl, family had always been second, and he'd expected the people who worked for him to feel the same way. Again she was reminded of all the problems they'd had before Dane's disappearance. But that wasn't important right now. Dane's recovery and reappearance was all that counted at the moment.

"Do you have a spare bed I can use?"

His question reinforced the barrier that had been slowly building up between them before he'd left for South America. She supposed it was a good idea not to share the same bedroom. He hadn't come right out and said it, but his meaning had been clear. They weren't the same two people as they had been when they had married. It wouldn't be fair to either one to put that kind of strain on their fragile relationship. "I don't have a spare bed, but the couch in the den makes up into a comfortable one."

"Thanks. I wasn't looking forward to staying in a motel." He took a step toward her. "I want to get to know you, Blake, Mandy…and Tara all over again. There are still parts of my life that are fuzzy, but I've been told being home will help."

She rose, the reality of their situation beginning to sink in. So much had happened in the past few years to both of them. The gulf between them at that moment seemed extremely wide. "Let me go talk with the children, tell them you're alive, then I'll bring them in here."

He peered down at his clothes as though checking to make sure he looked all right. The black pants and gray knit shirt hung off his frame. "Carl had someone buy these for me. He told me I'd fill them out in no time."

"Are you hungry?" Zoey gestured toward the kitchen. "I can fix you something to eat."

"Maybe later. I want to see the children."

Yes, first her children. How was she going to explain Dane's reappearance to them? "I won't be long."

A wry grin erased the worry in his expression. "I'm not going anywhere."

She returned his smile. "Are you sure you don't want something to eat? It's no trouble."

"I don't think I could eat right now."

Zoey looked at the lean lines of his face, the pallor beneath his tanned features, a tic that twitched in his jawline, and wanted to insist he eat something. He'd never liked her fussing over him in the past. She kept her mouth shut and headed toward the kitchen.

When she entered the room, her mother glanced up, concern carved into her expression. "Honey, is everything okay?" She lifted Tara from her high chair.

"Mandy, why don't you go in the den and watch TV with Blake for a few moments?"

After her daughter disappeared, Zoey turned to her mother, who held Tara in her arms. Her youngest played with her mother's dangling earring. "Mom, that stranger at the door was Dane."

Stunned, Emma sucked in a deep breath, her eyes round. "No!"

Zoey nodded. "He lost his memory when his plane crashed. Some Indians saved him. Until recently he hadn't remembered who he was."

Her mother shifted Tara to her other arm, burying her face in the toddler's hair. "But the government was sure he had died."

"The government made a mistake."

Emma moved toward Zoey. "Oh, honey." She took her into her arms with Tara between them. "What are you going to do?"

"Pick up the pieces of our marriage and start over. I need to tell Blake and Mandy now that their dad has returned from the dead."

"Do you want my help?"

Her mother had supported Zoey through some tough times after Dane had disappeared. Zoey moved back to her hometown because she'd realized she couldn't do it alone. After three months in Dallas trying to support her family financially and emotionally, she'd finally admitted she'd needed help and turned to her family and the Lord. She never regretted that choice. But right now she knew she had to do this alone, as so many things in the past few years.

"Just take care of Tara." Zoey lay her hand along her youngest child's jawline, feeling the softness beneath her palm. "At least you, my sweet, will be all right." She kissed Tara's cheek, then went to find her other two children.

In the den Zoey switched off the television, raising her hand to quiet the protests from Blake and Mandy. "We need to talk and I can't do that with the TV on." Sitting on the couch, Zoey patted the soft brown leather cushion. "Come here and sit with me."

Blake sat down next to her without a word while Mandy plopped down on the other side and bounced a few times as though testing the plumpness of the cushion. The whooshing sound permeated the silence. Zoey marveled at how much energy her daughter had after a long day playing and helping her get dinner ready.

"Mommy, who was that man?" Mandy finally settled next to her and looked up at her with her big, brown eyes that reminded Zoey so much of her own.

She didn't know where to begin. Blake had been nine when his father had left on his last assignment. And her five-year-old daughter hardly remembered the father who had been gone a lot that last year before he'd disappeared.

"Mom, is something wrong?" Blake asked, frowning.

"Mommy, did that man make you sad?" Mandy's mouth turned down in a frown, too, always imitating her older brother.

Zoey slipped her arms around her children and brought them close to her, savoring their nearness for a few seconds before she had to break the news. Mandy would be all right, but Zoey worried about Blake's reaction. He hadn't taken his father's death well, withdrawing into a shell for months after his father's disappearance. She'd tried to reach her son, but he was a lot like his father. He kept things bottled up inside.

Realizing she had been frowning herself while trying to find the best way to break the news to her children, Zoey forced a smile to her lips. "No, the man didn't make me sad. Not at all. In fact, just the opposite. I have some great news to share with you two." She drew in a deep breath and held it before releasing it through pursed lips. "The man Mandy is talking about is your father."

"Dad?" Blake pulled away, confusion knitting his brow. "But—I don't understand."

"Honey, your father has come home."

"Are you sure it's him? He didn't look like the pictures we have." Mandy hopped off the couch and faced Zoey, her face screwed up in a thoughtful expression as though she were picturing the man at the door and trying to reconcile in her mind that person with the photos she had of her father.

Both of her children peered at her as though she didn't have any idea what she was talking about. "Your father was believed to be dead, but he isn't. He's returned to us."

"Where was he? Why did he stay away? Why didn't he come home?" Blake asked, his voice rising as he bounded to his feet.

Zoey tried to grasp his hand, to tug him close to her. She wanted—needed—to hold him. Blake shuffled farther back, his scowl firmly in place. She didn't have all the answers for her son. She didn't know what had really happened and, knowing Dane, might never completely. All she could tell her children was what little she knew. "Your father was hurt and couldn't remember who he was until recently. He's in the living room waiting to see you two."

"Did he bring me a present?" Mandy asked,

hurrying toward the door. "Maybe he'll play a game with me or read me a story."

Zoey didn't have a chance to answer Mandy. She flew out of the room, leaving Zoey alone with her son, who looked as if he wasn't going to budge an inch.

"Honey, your father didn't choose to be gone for these past few years. As soon as he could, he came back to us." Drawing on her reserve of strength, Zoey stood and extended her hand toward Blake, noticing the slight tremor in her fingers. "Come talk to him, please." When her son didn't move, Zoey dropped her hand to her side and walked toward the door. "We'll be in the living room when you're ready."

For months after his father had disappeared, Blake had cried himself to sleep. He hadn't understood his father being gone for good. He'd wanted his playmate back—the man who rode him around on his shoulders, played ball with him, built sand castles at the beach with him. After the first year Blake had refused to discuss his father with anyone. She'd had the minister at their church and a counselor speak with Blake, but still he wouldn't talk about his father. Finally over time everything seemed to be back to normal. Now she wasn't so sure.

When she entered the living room, she found Mandy sitting next to Dane on the couch. Dane cradled Tara next to him, his eyes unusually bright as he took in first one daughter, then the other. Her mother had brought her youngest to meet her father.

Mandy stared at something cupped in her hand, wonder in her expression. She saw Zoey and leaped up, racing to her. "Look what he brought me. Coins from another country. They're different from ours. Look!" Mandy thrust them toward her.

Zoey picked up one and turned it over. "They're pretty."

"Yes." Her daughter closed her fingers around the coins and went back to Dane. "Thank ya. I'll put them with my other treasures." She stood in front of him now, not quite sure what to do.

Zoey came to her side. "Maybe you would like to show your father your treasure box."

A smile brightened her daughter's face. "I'll go get it." Mandy ran from the room and pounded up the stairs.

Zoey stared at the entrance into the living room, wondering if her son would appear. *Dear Lord, what should I do about Blake?* She chewed on her bottom lip and tried to think of what to tell Dane about their son.

"Mandy's full of life."

"That she is. There are days she can run me ragged." Zoey turned back to Dane, whose gaze was glued to his youngest daughter, as though he couldn't quite believe what he was seeing.

"She looks just like you, too. I'm glad. I wish I had known. I—"

The pain in his voice shredded the composure she'd fought hard to maintain for her children's sake. Her heart hammered against her chest, the beat vibrating in her head. Zoey peered at him and saw that glimpse of vulnerability she'd caught in his expression several times earlier. Sensing her regard, he quickly masked his look with a neutral one, something he was very good at doing. This was the Dane she knew—the one who didn't know how to share his feelings, who held a part of himself locked inside, the person her son was so similar to.

Exhausted from the past hour, Zoey collapsed in the chair next to the couch, wanting as much distance between them as possible in a room that had suddenly become small.

"Where's Blake?" Dane asked, his gaze fixed on the entrance into the living room.

"In the den."

"Is he coming in here?"

"No, I don't think so."

Dane tensed, the only indication that her words had affected him. "Why not?"

"When you...disappeared, Blake didn't take it well."

"But I'm here now. I know this isn't easy, but—"

Again that pain laced his voice and stabbed through her heart, through all the defenses she had erected. "But, what?" *Tell me what you're thinking,* she silently added.

Pressing Tara to him, he shuttered his look and rose. "I'll go have a word with him."

"Don't."

## Chapter Two

Dane froze. "What do you mean, don't? He's my son. I haven't seen him in over two years."

"I know." Zoey stood, her legs shaky. "When you didn't come home, he took your disappearance very hard. He cried for months, then clammed up and wouldn't say a word about you."

Dane closed his eyes for a few seconds, shaking his head. "Then he should be glad I'm back."

"He's—" she searched for a word that wouldn't be too harsh "—upset. I don't think Blake knows what to feel right now. Give him some time. He loves you very much. I think he's afraid you'll leave again for good."

"I need to see—" Dane clamped his jaws together and stared toward the entrance as though debating whether to ignore her advice or do as she had requested and give Blake some space.

"Please, Dane. I realize this is hard on you."

"Hard! I nearly died in that plane crash. If the Xingas hadn't found me and taken me in, I wouldn't be here. The first few months after the crash I was—" He snapped his mouth closed, gulped, then continued in a stilted voice, "I want to see my son, hold him." He buried his face in Tara's blond curls and breathed deeply while his daughter played with the buttons on his shirt between knuckling her eyes.

"So family is important to you now," Zoey said without thinking. She hadn't meant to add to his pain, but she had lived through Blake's silent suffering, through the years of watching Dane go off on one assignment after another, leaving her and the children alone to cope with his prolonged absences. But the worst was never knowing what was really going on with her husband.

Dane flinched. "Ouch. You're certainly blunt."

"Something I've learned to be over the last few years. A lot about me has changed."

"And a lot about me has changed."

"Then we aren't the same two people who married fourteen years ago?"

"No, and being strangers isn't a good foundation for a marriage."

"I agree. We have three children and we made a vow before God fourteen years ago that I intend to keep." Her emotions had gone through a roller-coaster ride tonight, as she was sure Dane's had as well, and she was too tired to get into a discussion about their future at this moment. She was glad when she heard Mandy pounding down the stairs.

Zoey's mother followed Mandy into the living room and took Tara from Dane. "Dane, I'm glad you're home safe. I'll get her ready for bed while you spend some time with Mandy."

"Thanks, Mom. She's starting to rub her eyes. Never a good sign." At Dane's questioning look, Zoey added, "When that happens, we have about half an hour to get Tara to bed before she falls apart. You don't want that. She can scream the roof off when she's tired enough."

With her treasure box clasped in her hands and a wide smile on her face, Mandy plopped down on the couch next to Dane and carefully opened the old pink-and-white gift box she'd received her last birthday. "See the rock I got when we went hikin'. And look at this coin Jesse and Nick gave me. That's when they went to—" Mandy peered at Zoey, her brow furrowed.

"To England."

"Yeah. Isn't it neat?" Mandy held the coin out in the palm of her hand for Dane to inspect.

"I loved different coins when I was a little boy. I had a collection."

Zoey blinked, surprised at what Dane had said. She hadn't known that. When she thought about it, Zoey realized she really didn't know a lot about Dane's childhood. Both his parents were dead, his mother from an illness. He had cared for his younger brother for a while, but he'd died when Dane was twenty-one. He'd refused to discuss his past, just as he'd refused to discuss his job. After years of asking, wanting to share his pain and help him, she had given up.

"Where's the coins?"

Dane cocked his head to the side and thought for a moment. "You know, Mandy, I'm not sure. I guess I lost them."

Mandy hugged the English coin. "I'll never lose my treasures."

Zoey listened to her daughter as she went through all her other prize possessions, cupping them in her small palm to show Dane, then letting him pick them up and examine them.

Zoey knew in that moment it wouldn't take long for Dane to win Mandy over.

Ten minutes later Mandy finished her presentation with a big yawn. "What'cha think of my treasures?"

"I can see why you take such good care of them."

"And it's time for bed, young lady. In fact, it's past your bedtime," Zoey said, a tightness in her throat from watching the exchange between Dane and Mandy.

"But, Mommy, I want to stay up and talk to Daddy."

"If you hurry, I'll tuck you in and read you your favorite story," Dane said, his words sounding thick, forced. He put the last treasure back in the box and closed its lid, his face averted.

Mandy leaped to her feet and without a backward glance rushed from the room. Dane still didn't look up.

Zoey chuckled, needing to ease the tension in the room. "Home less than an hour and she'll do anything you say. Of course, she loves for someone to read her favorite book to her. That's the only way I can get her into bed without an argument."

Finally Dane's shuttered gaze met hers. "What's her favorite book?"

"This month it's *Henrietta's Cat*. After she can recite it to you, her favorite book changes."

"I remember how Blake loved to be read to when he was her age."

The wistful tone in Dane's voice tugged at Zoey's heart. She wanted to comfort him, and yet a barrier stood between them that had slowly grown since he'd first arrived, a barrier that had been firmly in place the day he had left on his last assignment. It was as if they both began to remember the past and the problems still unsolved. An awkward silence fell between them. All Zoey heard was the ticking of the grandfather clock in the corner.

Dane cleared his throat, running his hand through his hair several times. "Well, I guess—" He rose, uncertainty in his expression.

"It'll take Mandy a few minutes to get ready. In the meantime, let me get some bedding for you." She started for the stairs. "I'm sure you're tired."

"Zoey, Carl said something about you being a counselor at Sweetwater High School."

"Yes, I had to do something to support the children. Our savings wasn't much, and you weren't legally declared dead yet, so I couldn't get the insurance. I love counseling the students and using my education. Now, I'd better get that bedding."

Zoey hurried up the stairs, leaving Dane alone with his turbulent thoughts. Zoey was a high school counselor. She had a whole other life without him. Her life had moved on while his had come to a screeching halt over two years ago. Memories bombarded him. He felt the heat of the fire. He heard the sounds of crunching metal. He squeezed his eyes closed and massaged his temples, trying to erase those aching memories, always just out of reach, never quite clear enough for him to piece the whole picture together.

A sound from the hallway drew his attention away from the past. He glimpsed Blake peering around the corner. He stepped toward his son. Blake darted past him and flew up the stairs. Dane wanted to go after him and pull him into his embrace, but the look on his son's face kept Dane rooted to the floor. The anger in Blake's expression made him realize Zoey was right. His son wasn't ready to accept him back into his life. Pain clawed at Dane's chest, constricting each breath as he inhaled deeply. Why had he thought it would be simple? That he would waltz right back into his old life and pick up where he'd left off? Did he even want that old life back? What did he want?

Dane scanned the living room and remembered a few pieces of furniture from when they'd lived in Dallas. But so much was different—the house, the town, his wife, his family. He'd desperately needed it to be the same, so he could completely reconstruct his life, fill in the few remaining holes in his memory. He felt the walls closing in on him.

He strode from the living room, fleeing out onto the porch as quickly as Blake had gone upstairs. Taking deep breaths of the crisp, spring air, Dane listened to the night silence around him. Somewhere in the distance a car started. A dog barked. The constriction in his chest eased.

He was in the United States, in Kentucky, Zoey's hometown. He wasn't in the rain forest any longer, trying to survive in an alien environment while trying to recover his health and remember. He was getting stronger each day. He had his memory back—mostly.

"Dane, are you all right?"

Zoey's worried voice penetrated his thoughts.

He needed to answer her, but his throat was tight with emotions he refused to acknowledge—was afraid to acknowledge.

"Dane? I saw Blake run to his room. Did you two talk?"

Frustrated, he pivoted, his arms stiff at his sides. "No, I didn't go against your wishes, if that's what you want to know. He ran past the living room and up the stairs before I could say a word to him."

"Give him some time. He'll come around." She hugged the bedding to her.

"And what about you and me?"

"I suspect we all need time to adjust to the changes."

"Because we aren't the same two people?"

"That and because we both remember what our marriage was like right before you left. A lot has happened to us in the past few years."

Weariness settled on his shoulders and laid heavily about him like the humidity in the jungle. He retrieved his duffel bag he'd put down before knocking on the screen door. "Here. Let me take those sheets and pillow. I can make up the bed. Just point me in the right direction."

Zoey moved to the side and gestured down

the hall. "The den is at the back of the house. When you're through, Mandy should be ready for a story."

He started past the entrance into the living room and paused. "Do you need any help?"

Zoey's brow creased. "Help?"

"Yes." He indicated the dishes still stacked on the dining room table from the family meal earlier. "I interrupted you cleaning up after dinner."

Zoey shook her head. "That's okay. It won't take me long. We ate late tonight because we'd been at my friend Darcy's farm. Mandy's taking riding lessons on Friday evenings and Blake had an extra soccer practice." She remembered the times they would clean up together, especially when they were first married, and how often they would end up in some kind of playful fight, sharing laughter, sharing a kiss. Those memories were too much for her at the moment because that had been a long time ago and a lot had happened since then.

"I'll read Mandy her story, then I'll look in on Tara. I'll wait on Blake. Which bedroom is his? I don't want to bother him and cause anymore trouble." Dane's voice was stiff and formal as though it was necessary to put a distance between them.

"The one with the closed door."

There was no expression on Dane's face as he headed toward the den to put up his duffel bag and bedding. The silence of the house, usually a balm, eroded what composure she had left. Moving into the living room, she sank onto a chair, hugging her arms to still the trembling that quickly spread throughout her body. Shudder after shudder left her vulnerable and uncertain what to do next. She buried her face in her hands and massaged her fingers into her temple. How was she going to keep her family together?

"Zoey?"

Her head snapped up, and she stared at her mother hovering over her. "I didn't hear you come in."

"Yes, I know."

"Is Tara in bed?"

"Yes, it took a while to get her to go down. Dane's saying good-night to her right now."

"He is? I didn't even see him go by."

"Maybe because you were deep in thought. Want to talk?"

Zoey rose slowly, weariness in every movement. "I'm all talked out, Mom."

"Are you sure? You look mighty lost."

"Oh, is it that obvious?"

"Yes, hon." Emma brushed Zoey's hair behind her ear. "Remember, I'm the one who you came to after Dane died—I mean, disappeared. Boy, this is hard. I've thought of him as being dead for so long. If I'm having a hard time, I know you are. What can I do to help?"

Tears misted Zoey's eyes. "You're doing it right now." She went into her mother's embrace, glad she'd come home when her life had been falling apart. Family and God were what was important. With them as her support she would be there for her children when they needed her.

"I tried to say good-night to Blake, but he was already asleep. That's the first time he's gone to bed before Mandy that I can remember. What happened in the den? Did he talk to Dane?"

Zoey pulled back, one tear rolling down her cheek, then another. "No. He was so upset that Dane was here that he wouldn't talk to his father. What should I do?"

"Pray. Have faith that God will help you through this. He was there for you in the past. He is here for you now, and He will be there for you in the future."

Zoey swiped her hand across her cheeks. "I'm happy that Dane is alive, Mom, but my world is suddenly no longer the safe haven I've worked so hard to make it. Everything's changed tonight."

Emma gripped Zoey's hands. "No, it hasn't. Your faith is the same. Your love for your children and family is the same. Keep that in mind." She scanned the mess in the dining room. "Now, let me give you a hand cleaning this up."

"No, you've done enough. I won't be able to sleep for a while. You go home and get some rest. I'll talk to you tomorrow."

"You always did like to be alone to wrestle with your problems. That hasn't changed, I see." Her mother squeezed Zoey's hands before releasing them and making her way toward the front door. "I expect to hear from you before the sun sets tomorrow."

"I'm surprised you don't want me to call you before the sun rises."

"Hon, for once I think I'll be sleeping late. Good night."

The sound of the front door closing echoed through the house. Zoey stared at it for a moment, feeling all her uncertainty crashing down on her. Dane was finally home and a few feet away in the same house. Her children were upstairs, safe. All should be well with the world, and yet she felt the fabric of her life unraveling.

She headed up the stairs, needing to check on her children before cleaning up. She stood at Mandy's door and listened to Dane read to her. Her daughter was curled up next to him, her eyes drooping closed. Next, Zoey went to Tara's room and kissed her sleeping toddler's forehead. Then she opened Blake's door and peeked into his room. The light from the hallway shone across his bed. Her son lay buried under mounds of blankets as though he were trying to shut the world out. In that moment she had the same urge.

She walked to her bedroom and retrieved her Bible by her bed. Sitting in a chair by the window, she opened the book and sought comfort in its pages.

*Dear Heavenly Father, I don't know if I can do what I need to do. Help me to make this marriage work, to find the strength to make us a whole family again. I am lost and afraid of what the future holds. Please show me the way.*

*The dank darkness surrounded him as though he were wearing a straightjacket. The pain gnawed at his insides, consuming his whole body. The heat pressed down on him, making it difficult to breathe. Tight. Suffocating— He reached out. Fire licked at his fingers, searing his flesh.*

With a gasp Dane opened his eyes and found a gray-and-black cat balanced on his chest, two blue eyes staring at him. A cat? Where was he? Confusion clouded his mind, the fragments of his reoccurring nightmare lingering in his thoughts.

The animal lifted his paw and batted at Dane's face. He scrambled to sit up.

"What in the world—"

"That's Pepper, our cat."

Dane snapped his head around to find Mandy sitting by the couch staring at him. He was in Sweetwater, Kentucky. Zoey's house. *I'm okay.* He shoved the nightmare to the back recesses of his mind.

"He's my pet. Blake doesn't like him."

"He doesn't?"

"He wanted a dog, but I found Pepper, cryin' outside in the front yard. He was wet and hungry. No one claimed him so we kept him." Mandy perched on the side of the bed and bounced a few times. "Do ya want to play a game?"

Pepper rubbed his body against Dane's chest, then nudged his hand. "How about after breakfast?" Dane glanced at his watch and saw that it was early. "Is anyone else up?"

"Oh, yes. Mommy's takin' a bath. She likes to do that sometimes instead of a shower. She's been in the bathroom a loo-oong time."

Dane decided if he ever wanted to know what was going on in the family all he had to do was ask Mandy. "Let me get dressed and see if I can get some coffee started. Maybe you can help me."

"Sure." She jumped to her feet and scooped Pepper up into her arms. "I'll be in the kitchen. I don't know if we have any coffee. Mommy doesn't drink it."

"She still drinks tea?"

"Yep." Mandy said, walking slowly from the den.

That was one of the many differences Zoey and he'd had. One of the first things he'd requested when he'd returned to civilization was a large mug of brewed coffee. Before the plane crash, he'd drunk at least five cups a day. After the crash, he hadn't been able to remember what he liked for a long time. Even if he had, coffee hadn't been on the menu in the Indian village where he'd stayed.

Dane used the bathroom off the den, quickly shaving and showering. When he entered the kitchen, he found Zoey putting a kettle of water on the stove. Mandy sat at the table, eating a bowl of cereal with bananas. When she saw him, she beamed at him, revealing her missing front tooth.

"We have to put Pepper out in the backyard when we eat. He likes to get up on the table and stick his nose into my food. No matter how many times we put him on the floor, he gets back up. Mommy finally gave up tryin' to teach him not to get up on the table."

Zoey turned from the stove, a flushed cast to her cheeks. Her long blond hair was tied back in a ponytail while her brown eyes stared at him with a wariness that he'd seen a lot in the last months before his disappearance.

"I have some instant coffee somewhere in here." She opened several cabinet doors and found the jar.

He winced.

"Instant is all I can offer you."

"Maybe I can go to the Quick Mart on the corner and get some real coffee."

"Sorry. I don't have a coffeepot anymore."

"What happened to it?"

"I gave it away after—" A frown flitted across her features.

"Never mind. Instant will be fine."

"I'll get a pot today at the super center."

"That's okay. I can take care of it. I don't want to put you out."

"Nonsense. You're our guest—" She swallowed her next words. "I mean—"

Dane held up his hand. "I understand, Zoey. Really. This isn't a normal situation. I don't want you to go to any trouble."

"It's no trouble. I'm going to the store anyway." She snatched up the kettle as it began to whistle and poured hot water into two mugs.

Her hand shook. They sounded like polite strangers instead of husband and wife, she thought, and stirred the coffee granules into his mug, then gave it to him.

"I'll go with you to the store. There are some things I want to pick up." Dane took a sip of his coffee and kept his expression neutral.

Zoey dunked her tea bag into her hot water, then spooned in some honey. "We'll go after breakfast."

"Mommy, Daddy was gonna play a game with me."

"He can later. Blake has a soccer game this morning and I want to get the shopping done before the game."

Mandy drew her brows together and formed a pout. "We always have to go to his games. Can I stay at Nana's with Tara?"

"I guess so if it's okay with her," Zoey said, bringing her mug to the table and placing it on the mat across from Dane's.

"Call her. Call her!"

"Not until you've cleaned your room and made your bed, young lady."

Mandy hurriedly finished her cereal in two bites and raced from the room before Zoey could say anything.

Dane chuckled. "I didn't know it was possible to eat so fast."

"Mandy does everything on fast mode. She'll be back down here in a few minutes, declaring her room is clean. Of course, when I go up to inspect it, most of the items on the floor will be shoved under her bed. She'll moan and groan, but finally pull them all out and put them where they belong."

"If she knows you're gonna check, why doesn't she put them away the first time?"

Zoey shrugged. "I think she's an eternal optimist. She's just sure one day I won't check."

"She sounds like she's gotten more than her looks from you."

"I've tempered my optimism with realism. When life slaps you in the face, it's hard not to." Zoey sipped at her tea, glad to have something to do with her hands. "Would you like some cereal? I know you like a big breakfast, but the only morning I have time to fix one is Sunday before we go to church."

"I'm not used to having a big breakfast anymore. Where's the cereal?"

"You mean cereals." She pointed to the cabinet next to the refrigerator. "When you have three hungry children, we go through several boxes in a week. I do have some that aren't laced with tons of sugar."

"Actually sugar sounds good. I've missed it."

An uncomfortable silence fell between them as Dane prepared his bowl of cereal topped with a banana. Zoey wanted to ask him about his years in the jungle, about his lost memory, but after the night before, she knew he wouldn't say anything to her until he was ready, if ever. She didn't want him to reject confiding in her a second time. Her battered emotions could only take so much.

Dane settled again in the chair across from her and dug into his cereal. When he was halfway finished, he looked up and speared her with his intense gaze. "Where's Blake? I'd hoped to see him this morning."

Zoey glanced at the clock over the desk. "He should have been down by now. I'd better go see what's keeping him. He's supposed to go over to Nate's this morning before the game. I need to check on Tara, too. She should be up. I usually hear her by now."

Zoey hurried up the stairs, stopping by Mandy's room to see how she was progressing with her cleanup. With a quick look under her daughter's bed, then the closet, Zoey shook her head and said, "You're gonna have to try harder if you want to go to Nana's this morning." There was a part of her that hoped Mandy didn't accomplish her task, the part that didn't want to be alone with Dane, the part that was confused and not sure what to do.

"Oh, Mommy. Everything's off the floor."

"Yeah, and this time stuffed in your closet."

"But it's not under the bed."

Zoey put her hands on her hips and fixed a stern expression on her face. "Young lady, you know what a clean room is supposed to be like."

Next Zoey went to Blake's room and knocked on the closed door. When she didn't hear anything, she knocked again, louder.

Suddenly the door swung open. He was still dressed in his pajamas with his hair sticking up at odd angles as though he had just rolled out of bed. He knuckled sleep from his eyes.

"You need to hurry and come down to breakfast before you go to Nate's."

"I'm not hungry," he mumbled, his gaze dropping away from hers.

"You need to eat something. You've got a soccer game later this morning."

"I'll get dressed and walk over to Nate's. It's only five blocks."

"You can't avoid your dad, Blake."

He scowled. "Yes, I can."

Her son started to close his door, but Zoey stuck her foot in the doorway to stop him. "Your father is here to stay."

"How do you know?"

His question caught her off guard. She didn't know for sure. Dane's job with the DEA had always been so important to him, to the point that she'd felt her and their family had often come in second. He'd told her the evening before he didn't have plans yet, but if past patterns were any indication, Dane would be gone on some DEA assignment as soon as he felt he had recovered, and Blake needed a full-time father, especially right now. "I want you downstairs for breakfast in ten minutes."

She didn't wait for her son to protest her command. She hurried to Tara's room and found her youngest playing in her crib as though she had been patiently waiting for someone to come get her. It wouldn't be long before she needed to put the crib away and get a big girl bed for Tara. Her youngest was growing up too fast.

"Sweet pea, time to get up."

With a big smile, Tara stood in the crib and lifted her arms for Zoey to take. "Mama, up now."

After quickly changing Tara's diaper and dressing her, Zoey carried her downstairs, noticing her son's bedroom door was still closed. Blake was a good kid. He'd do what he needed to do.

As she entered the room, Dane placed his bowl in the dishwasher, then poured himself another cup of coffee. She drew in a deep breath at the sight of him in her kitchen. She'd never thought she would see that again. Then she remembered Blake's question about Dane staying and needed a more definite answer than the one Dane had given her the night before.

"What are your plans, Dane?" Zoey put Tara

into her high chair, then tied a bib around her neck. She gave her daughter some apple juice to drink in a sippy cup.

He glanced up, his eyebrows rising. "To go with you to the store."

"No, I mean for your future." She heard the exasperation in her voice and didn't care. She was frustrated, confused and afraid for her children, for herself.

A shadow dimmed his eyes before he veiled his expression and focused his attention on his mug of coffee. "I told you last night, I haven't made any plans yet. That hasn't changed in the past ten hours. I just got back to the States not long ago."

"How long have you been back?"

"Five days."

"Five days! Why did it take so long to let me know you were alive?" She was determined not to feel hurt, but it gripped her in its powerful talons.

"Zoey, I wasn't in the best of shape. The jungle can be hard on a person's body. I was in a hospital, then I had to be debriefed."

"Hospital!" She collapsed into a chair next to Dane, her whole body trembling. "I should have been there."

"I didn't want our reunion to be in a hospital

and Carl wanted me to be checked out thoroughly before leaving Dallas. I even had to see a psychologist."

"How many people knew you were back before I did?" she asked, the hurt she couldn't keep at bay lacing her question. Again she was reminded that she had often come in second to his job.

His gaze snared hers, dark, hard and unreadable. "Not many. I didn't want the media to get a hold of it before I had a chance to see you."

"Thank you for that." Zoey gripped the table's edge and leaned into it. "I still want to know what your plans are. Where do Blake, Mandy, Tara and I fit into your life?"

He hesitated, taking a long sip of his coffee.

His silent wall was in place. She might have changed in the past two years, but Dane really hadn't. He was still quite good at shutting her out of his life. "Never mind. That says it all."

He finally pierced her with that probing look of his. "Says what? That I'm not sure what I'm going to do? That I've spent the past few years wondering who I am? That I'm still trying to fill in some gaps in my memory?"

Her anger fizzled as quick as it surfaced. "What gaps?"

"I don't remember anything leading up to the

crash and right afterwards. They tell me Bob Patterson, my partner, was on the plane. I don't remember any of that. So you see, I haven't had time to decide what I'm going to do."

She didn't want to add to Dane's pain, but she had her son to think about, too. Blake was hurting. "Blake's worried you'll leave soon." *And so I am,* she silently added.

"I'm not—"

The door eased opened, and her son came into the room, a pout on his face, his eyes downcast. He plodded to the cabinet and prepared himself some cereal, then started eating it at the counter.

"Blake, please have a seat," Zoey said in a gentle voice, aware how fragile her son's emotions were at the moment because they mirrored hers.

"I'm fine," he mumbled, his attention trained on his bowl as though it were the most delicious food he'd ever had.

Zoey scooted back the chair next to her. "We don't eat at the counter. We sit down as a family at the table."

He huffed, then grabbed his bowl and trudged to the table where he plopped into the chair. Not once did he look toward Dane. But his father watched him, a sadness in his eyes that ripped apart Zoey's fragile control. Putting her family back together wouldn't be easy. Like Humpty Dumpty, the nursery rhyme she often read to Tara, it might never be accomplished.

Silence, thick and heavy, lay like a blanket over the room. Zoey swallowed several times to coat her parched throat, searching for something to say to ease the tension. Nothing came to mind.

"Blake, I hear you have a soccer game later this morning. What position do you play?" Dane asked, cupping his mug between his hands and bringing it to his lips.

"Forward," her son mumbled, barely audible.

"I used to play in high school and college. I was the goalie."

Blake continued to eat his cereal, his movements quickening as if he couldn't finish fast enough. Finally he spooned the last bite into his mouth and shot to his feet. "Mom, may I get ready to go to Nate's?"

Zoey nodded, her throat constricted.

After putting his bowl in the sink, Blake hurried from the kitchen. Zoey looked at Dane, wishing there was something she could do to make the situation better between father and son.

"I didn't do it on purpose, you know," Dane said into the quiet that again reigned.

"What?"

"Be gone for two-and-a-half years."

"It's more than that, Dane. He thought you had died. He had to deal with those emotions and now he realizes that wasn't really what happened. He didn't handle it very well then and I'm afraid he might not handle it very well now."

"And what about you?"

## Chapter Three

"Are you asking me if I handled your 'death' well?" Zoey remembered the days of numbness, of not feeling as though she could get a handle on anything, and never wanted to revisit that time—not even in her memories. Despite often coming in second in Dane's life, hers had revolved around him. His disappearance had shaken the very foundation of her life to the point she'd had to grapple with who she was.

"I suppose I am." One corner of Dane's mouth hitched up in a self-mocking smile that reminded her so much of the old Dane, self-assured of every move he made.

"I'd rather not talk about the past right now," was all she could say.

"I guess I deserve that."

She didn't want to reveal the depth of her despair. That would leave her open to being hurt by Dane all over again, and she wouldn't allow that to happen—once was enough. She shoved back her chair and rose. "I'd better get Tara fed, then we need to leave if we're going to get any shopping done before the soccer game."

"I'm eager to see Blake play. I just wish he was eager for me to see him play."

"Give him time. He'll come around."

"I hope you're right. It's been a while since I've been a father."

The wistful tone in Dane's voice bothered her more than she cared to acknowledge. "It's like riding a bike. If you fall, you can pick yourself up and try again." Zoey prepared Tara's breakfast, then started to sit and feed her.

Dane waved her away, taking the spoon and dipping it into the cereal. "I'll do this."

She glanced about her, needing something to do. She couldn't just stand there and stare at Dane feeding their youngest daughter. Watching him with Tara brought emotions to the surface she wasn't ready to deal with. How many times had she wished for this very thing? She had prayed for Dane to be a part of the children's lives—her life— again, but how long would this last? Their discussion of what he was going to do underscored all the reasons she should guard her heart from further pain. He had broken it once before, and she had finally patched it together. She couldn't go through that anguish again. Zoey began cleaning up what few dishes remained, then placed a call to her mother to make sure it was all right for Mandy to join Tara.

When Dane was finished, he wiped Tara's face and hands, then lifted her from the high chair. "We're all ready."

Zoey scooped up Tara's dishes and placed them in the sink to take care of later. "Then let's go." *I need to be around people,* she thought and headed for the front of the house. At the bottom of the stairs she called, "Blake. Mandy, it's time to go."

Mandy bounded down the stairs with one of her dolls clutched in her hand. "Nana's making some clothes for Mrs. Giggles. They should be ready today." She raced out onto the porch, leaving the front door wide open.

At a much more sedate pace Blake came down the steps, dressed in his soccer uniform, his head bowed, his shoulders slumped, as though he were going to do something he hated to do. But Zoey knew he loved to play soccer, which made his demeanor even more worrisome. She wished she could erase his troubles and make everything all right. But life wasn't that simple, and her son was going to hurt because of that. Again she felt a helplessness—any control she had over her future gone.

When Blake reached the bottom, Zoey laid her hand on his shoulder, intending to draw him into an embrace, to let him know she would be with him every step of the way. He wrenched away and hurried toward the car.

"I'm sorry, Zoey. I know this can't be easy for you, either."

She looked at Dane, saw his usual neutral expression in place and struggled to keep her anger in line. What would it take for him to open up to her? Was it even possible for him to share himself totally with another person? How was this marriage going to survive when they really didn't know each other anymore? How was she going to forgive Dane when he kept a part of himself shut off from her still? Not trusting her enough to share his innermost thoughts? Nothing had really changed in their marriage since he'd been gone. She remembered the desperation and sadness she'd felt right before his last assignment. It came to the foreground, demanding attention.

"It's hard watching someone you care about hurting," she finally said and followed her children to the car.

Zoey dropped Mandy and Tara off first at her mother's house, then Blake at Nate's. The silence in the car after the girls left was nerve-racking. Zoey flipped on the radio to fill it, but nothing lessened the tension churning in her stomach.

When she pulled into a parking space at the super center, she quickly exited the car and hurried toward the store. Suddenly she needed some distance, which thankfully Dane gave her for a few minutes. His nearness caused so many conflicting emotions to surface that it was hard to grasp onto any one feeling for long.

She waited for him with her shopping cart inside the door. Slowly he made his way toward her, his gaze intense as it bore into her. She had no idea what was going on in his mind. And to think about what he must have endured the past few years made her heart throb painfully. What she'd said to him before leaving the house was as much about him as Blake.

She gave him a tentative smile to try and ease the strain in their strange situation. She felt the corners of her mouth quiver from the effort, but she managed to maintain the smile. "I need to pick up some odds and ends. If you want to meet me back here, we can check out together."

For a good minute he didn't say anything. He scanned the rows and rows of items and for a fleeting few seconds a bewildered look entered his eyes. "I'd forgotten how big these stores are. I'll come with you. I just need a few personal items."

"We'll pick up the coffeepot first."

"You won't get a complaint from me."

"I noticed you didn't eat much breakfast. That was usually such an important meal for you. Is there anything I can get you for breakfast?" she asked, needing to fill any silence between them with idle chatter. The silence allowed her to think, which had been the main reason she had tossed and turned the past night—that and the fact Dane was only a few rooms away. Those few rooms might as well be a continent.

Again Dane didn't respond right away. Zoey slanted a look at him and noticed the tightening about his mouth. She didn't know what to say to him—what was a good topic for conversation.

"I'm sorry, Dane, if—"

He shook his head. "You have nothing to be sorry about."

Uncomfortable, Zoey wheeled the cart toward the small appliance area.

"My love for coffee hasn't diminished. I just haven't gotten the chance to indulge like I used to. In fact, I haven't indulged in much lately. I must say, what the jungle had to offer is quite different from what this store has to offer. Makes you appreciate the small things we take for granted."

Even though he sounded cavalier, her throat ached with suppressed feelings. His closed expression prohibited further discussion. He'd always insisted he kept quiet about his work to protect her. He'd never understood she'd needed to share the bad as well as the good with him.

She compelled herself to smile. "Then after we shop here, I know a store that sells the best coffee in this part of Kentucky. We'll have to hurry, though. We don't have much time before the game."

"Why, Zoey, it's so good to see you. I heard the news. Is this your young man?" Susan Daniels, her mother's best friend, asked, planting herself in their path, her sharp, assessing gaze on them.

Zoey knew they wouldn't be going any-where until they had satisfied the older woman's curiosity. "Susan, this is my husband, Dane Witherspoon."

He nodded, a finely honed tension emanating from him. "Pleased to meet you."

"My, what a ruckus you've caused in this little town, young man. Coming back from the dead. You must tell us what happened sometime."

Dane stiffened. "There's not much to tell."

Waves of tension rolled off Dane. Zoey stepped between him and Susan. "I wish we had more time to talk, but Blake has a soccer game in less than an hour and we still have a lot of shopping to do. We'll have to chat another time." She maneuvered her cart around the older woman and continued toward the small appliance aisle, hoping Susan Daniels didn't follow.

"You can slow down now, Zoey. I think we lost her at ladies' clothing," Dane said behind her.

Zoey glanced back. "Are you sure? When Susan wants to know something, she's ruthless in her pursuit."

"Then she's met her match," Dane said with a thread of steely determination she'd heard on more than one occasion.

She stopped in the middle of the small appliance aisle. "You have to realize, Dane, that everyone will want to know all the details."

"It's none of their business."

"But that's the way small towns are, especially since you never came with me and the children to visit Mom. You're a mystery to them."

"My past is just that, in the past."

Realizing the people of Sweetwater had truly met their match in Dane, Zoey grabbed a box from the shelf. "I need a few cleaning supplies and some cat litter. Then we can get your things and get out of here."

"It doesn't bother you?"

"What?"

"People wanting to know your private affairs."

"Sure, but you get used to it. There are some good things about small towns."

"What?"

"I'm not alone. If I have a problem, there's always someone around to help me."

"Is that why you moved back here?"

"Yes. It wasn't easy, but like you, I'd just as soon not discuss it. We can both have our secrets." Which she knew wasn't a good basis for a marriage, but she was determined to protect herself. Being the only one opening up in a relationship wasn't good. She'd lived through that kind of relationship once before, and she wouldn't do it again.

They quickly finished shopping and checked out. Walking to the car, Zoey was aware of people watching them, a few whispering to the person next to them. The people of Sweetwater meant well and cared about her and her family, but their interest was making the situation even more awkward than it already was.

At the car she said, "I forgot to ask earlier. You can drive if you want."

His eyes clouded. "No, I'm not familiar with the town yet, and it has been a while since I was behind the wheel of a car."

Dane had always insisted on driving before. He didn't like anyone else driving when he was in the car. This change surprised Zoey, but she kept her thoughts to herself as she backed out of the parking space and headed toward the coffee shop on Second Street.

"You can wait in the car. I'll get this," Dane said as though he needed to show his independence.

Zoey watched her husband walk into the shop, say a few words to the lady behind the counter, then wait for her to fill his order. Zoey took deep breaths, but her chest still felt tight. Again, the feeling they were only polite strangers assailed her. How did they get past that? She couldn't see going through the rest of her life skirting certain issues, pretending nothing was wrong when everything was.

*Please, Lord, I feel so lost. I need Your help. What do I do now?*

Nothing came to mind. Her shoulders slumped, and she rested her forehead on the steering wheel. She felt like the Hebrews wandering in the desert looking for their home. Lost. Alone. Miles and miles of barren land before her.

The sound of the door opening jolted her, and she straightened. Dane slid into the front seat, his expression unreadable.

"Dane, before we get to the soccer fields, I want you to know there will be a lot of people there and they'll be curious about you and what happened. A few may even ask questions."

"I can't stop them from asking." A half grin slipped across his mouth. "Thanks for warning me."

"They'll mean well."

"I know."

"They'll just be concerned about me."

"And they don't think I am?"

Her grip on the steering wheel strengthened

until pain shot up her arms. "To tell you the truth, I don't know what you think anymore. Everything has changed." She started the car and pulled out onto the road.

A heavy silence greeted that declaration. Tension mounted in the car, and it took all Zoey's concentration to keep herself focused enough to drive to the soccer fields. She felt as though she were in an intense struggle—for her marriage, for her future—all in the span of fifteen hours.

"I know, but—" He couldn't complete his sentence, his words dissolving into that uncomfortable silence.

She parked the car. "It looks like Blake's game is about to start. We'd better hurry."

"I'll be along in a sec," came Dane's clipped response.

She climbed from the car and strode toward the bleachers, feeling the drill of Dane's gaze into her back. A shiver flashed up her spine, and she rubbed her arms. Still the cold embedded itself deep in her bones. She sat next to Jesse Blackburn and offered her friend a smile that died instantly.

"Your mother called me and told me everything." Jesse took her hand and squeezed it.

Zoey pictured her mom on the phone all morning before they had dropped off the girls, spreading the news to Zoey's circle of friends that Dane had returned from the dead.

"I know it can't be easy for you. Anytime you want to talk I'm here for you. We all are—Darcy, Beth, Tanya."

"I know." Zoey gulped, trying to dislodge the lump in her throat that made speaking difficult.

"I'll try to fend off these vultures." Jesse glanced around her.

"Shh," Zoey said with a shaky laugh. "Don't say that too loud."

"It's true. They've all been waiting for you to come. Your mom said it didn't go well with Blake."

Zoey found her son on the field with Alex Stone, the high school principal, who coached her son's team. "No, it didn't."

"Honey, I'm sorry. I wish I could do something to make it all better."

Alex clasped Blake on the shoulder and leaned down to say something to her son. Zoey dragged her gaze away from the pair, praying one day that Dane and Blake would regain the close relationship they'd once had. "My problem now is how do I make this all better for my son."

"Be there for him. Like you were when you thought he'd lost his father."

A deep sigh escaped Zoey's lips. She remembered the long struggle after Dane's disappearance with Blake resisting any attempt at help. A bone-tired weariness blanketed her as she thought of the path ahead of her—and Dane.

Her husband was back, but for how long? It had taken her a long time to learn to stand on her own two feet after he'd disappeared. She'd married Dane right after college and had never really been on her own until she'd been forced to with his disappearance. Over the past few years she had slowly learned to depend only on herself. She would hold this family together somehow, but she would keep her heart guarded.

Dane eased down next to her. She wanted to take his hand and hold it, to convey her support, to begin to forge a future for them, but his closed expression stopped her. She trained her gaze on the field to watch the start of the game, the tension between her and Dane razor sharp. He had pulled into himself even further. She suspected to protect himself. It was something he was quite good at doing. And it was something she was going to have to learn to do if she was going to survive this upheaval.

Toward the end of the first half Dane leaned close and whispered, "The coach is very good with our son."

"Yes, Alex is. Blake can count on him."

"But not me?"

Zoey pulled back and looked long and hard at Dane. "I didn't say that."

"You didn't have to. I wasn't there for Blake when he obviously needed it. I'm glad someone was. I just wished it had been me."

This time she did take his hand. "So do I."

"But it wasn't me, Zoey."

"Dane—"

He forced a smile to his lips. "Maybe I should ask this Alex for pointers. I'm certainly going to need them with my own son."

Suddenly Zoey felt conscious of the people around them listening to their conversation. She pressed her lips together and resolved to pursue this discussion later even if Dane's expression was now cloaked, as though he regretted that brief glimpse of vulnerability.

At the half, the people around them introduced themselves to Dane and welcomed him to Sweetwater. He evaded their questions about where he had been and what he had been doing. Keeping secrets, holding himself apart from others, came so effortlessly and naturally to him that Zoey didn't know if he could truly be a member of a family or a small town like Sweetwater.

When Wilbur Thompson kept wanting to know what he'd been up to these last few years, Zoey knew living in a small town was going to propose a lot of problems for Dane. Dallas had suited him well because he could get lost in a crowd. Sweetwater would eat him up alive because many people like Wilbur didn't take no comment for an answer.

Finally Dane looked Wilbur in the eye and said, "I can't help you, Mr. Thompson."

Wilbur opened his mouth to pursue the subject, stared at the diamond-hard expression in Dane's eyes, and clamped his lips together with a snort. The older man went back to sit at the top of the bleachers next to his wife, clearly not pleased that his curiosity hadn't been appeased.

Zoey was thankful when the second half started, and everyone sat down again. Jesse decided to join Dane on the other side of him so he was between her and Zoey.

"Just in case anyone else wants to pry. They'll have to crawl over me to get to you,"

Jesse whispered, loud enough that many of the people heard. A few laughed.

"I thank you for your assistance. I didn't relish getting into a fight the first day in town, especially with a man thirty years my senior."

"And since Wilbur's son is the police chief, it probably wouldn't be a good idea. That man thinks everyone's business is his. He fancies himself an amateur detective because of his son's profession. He says it runs in his genes."

"Is that a warning?"

"Well, I guess it is. Wilbur's son, Zach, even tried to court Zoey a while back. Finally he gave up. He's not like his daddy. He knows when to cut his losses and move on, thank goodness."

Zoey was wondering if she could stuff a sock in her friend's mouth. Jesse was way too informative, but then she always knew what was going on in Sweetwater, sometimes before the people involved.

Dane grinned. "I know that if I need any help you're the one to come to."

"Yep. I've always been there for Zoey. Been her friend since grade school. We lost touch when she was in Dallas, but now that she's back, we've picked up where we left off as though a day hasn't passed. I'm the one who encouraged her to apply for the counseling job at the high school. She needed something to do and she's really good at helping the students."

"Jesse," Zoey cut in, "how's your son doing?"

Jesse leaned around Dane, a puzzled expression on her face. "Zoey, he's right there on the field next to Blake. He's fine."

"Yes, I see. But didn't you say he was having trouble with his ears?"

Jesse waved her hand. "That was last week. He's on medication again for another ear infection, but he's much better."

Dane straightened, his attention focused on Blake moving down the field toward the goal. Their son paused, aimed and kicked the ball. It shot toward the goal. The goalie dove for it but missed it by a few inches. Both Zoey and Dane leaped to their feet, cheering when the ball sailed between the goal posts for a score.

"He's good," Dane said, beaming at Zoey.

"He loves to play ever since he moved here. You should have seen him that first year. He—" The look of pain that flashed across Dane's face halted her words. "I'm sorry. I shouldn't have said anything."

"No, I'm the one who is sorry. I want you to feel free to talk about what our children have done in the past. How else will I get to know them now if you don't?" He moved in close and continued in a low voice, "The same goes for you and what you've been doing. It was nice listening to what Jesse had to say. It makes me realize you and I need to spend some time alone talking about what you've done the past few years."

*What I've been doing, but not you?* His presence overpowered her, her senses inundated with his nearness. Zoey wanted to back away from Dane, but she didn't. She didn't want the townspeople to hear any of their conversation. "Will you share your life for the past few years, too?"

A shadow furrowed his brow. "There's really nothing to share. I survived the crash and finally remembered who I was. I lived with good people who took me in. I learned to live in an environment very different from here without any trappings of civilization."

She touched his arm, vaguely aware that people were staring at them, that the soccer game had continued. She didn't care. "Sharing that is a beginning." She sat, and Dane sat next to her on the bench. "I think your idea about talking is a good one. I'll see if Mom can watch the children tonight. We can go out to dinner."

"A date?"

"Yes. We may be married, but there's so much we don't know about each other."

"Zoey, don't expect me—"

She took his hand, stopping his words. "We have to start somewhere. For the children's sake."

"How about our own?"

His question, unanswered, hung in the air between them. Zoey wanted to hope one day they could capture the emotions they'd had when they'd first married before real life had intruded, before his work had taken him away from her and thrown up a wall between them that she couldn't seem to scale, even now. But she was a realist now, and she didn't know if that was possible.

Mandy clapped. "I won! I won!"

Dane began to put the pieces of the board game back in the box. "Did anyone ever tell you how lucky you are, young lady?"

"Yes, Mommy all the time." Mandy helped to clean up the mess. "Ya look nice."

He ran his finger under his collar. "You think so? I haven't worn a suit and tie in a long time."

"Is this what ya bought today at the store, Daddy?"

Every time his daughter called him "daddy" his heart swelled. How could he have forgotten her—forgotten Zoey and Blake? Oh, he knew all the medical reasons for amnesia, but in his heart he should have known. Guilt gnawed at his insides for the lost years.

He cleared his throat before replying, "I figured I'd better get some clothes that fit me."

"I want to go out with ya and Mommy to eat." Mandy came to sit next to him on the couch. "I have a pretty new dress that Nana bought me. I can wear it."

His first impulse was to tell her yes. She would be a good buffer between him and Zoey. But he'd never been a coward before, and he wasn't going to start now. He placed his arm around Mandy's shoulder and pulled her against him. "You can another time. Your mother and I need to talk."

"That's okay. Ya can talk. I won't mind."

"Sometimes grown-ups need time alone. Just like you and I need special time alone."

Mandy pouted. "Okay. This time. And I'll give ya a chance to beat me tomorrow."

"That's a date. Just you and me."

He hugged her, relishing the feel of his daughter in his arms. He'd missed so much with her. Regret mixed with anger, always beneath the surface, surged in him, threatening his composure. Clenching his hands, he closed his eyes and forced those emotions to the dark recesses of his mind before they overwhelmed him. He'd survived the plane crash when no one else had. He'd finally made it back to his family. He was remembering new things every day. He would get his life back. He had to!

When the doorbell rang, he used that as an excuse to leave Mandy. In the hallway, he took several deep breaths to fortify himself. A feeling of helplessness, one he'd dealt with many times in the rain forest, nibbled at his mind. He pushed that away, too. He would never feel helpless again. He would control his own life from now on. He knew who he was and that was half the battle. The rest would fall into place now that he was home again.

Composed, Dane opened the door to allow Emma into the house. "Thanks for helping out on such short notice."

"My pleasure. Anything for Zoey and you." She placed her purse on the table in the foyer. "Where are the children?"

"Blake's in his room, has been since he came home from the game. Tara's with Zoey. And

Mandy just beat me at a board game. She's quite a competitor."

"Even though she looks like Zoey, there's a lot of you in her."

Dane smiled.

Emma glanced up the stairs. "After you and Zoey leave, I'll go up and talk with Blake."

"Good luck. Zoey tried to and he didn't say two words."

"Where's Zoey?"

"Still getting dressed, I think."

At that moment Dane saw Zoey at the top of the stairs, her gaze fixed on him. He sucked in a deep breath and held it while she walked down the steps, carrying their youngest child. His wife looked gorgeous in a simple black dress with a lace shawl draped over her. Her outfit fell to her knees and accentuated her long legs clad in black hose. Her shoulder-length blond hair was swept back from her face, emphasizing her big, brown eyes. Around her neck she wore a white gold chain with a single black pearl that he'd given her on their first anniversary. The memory pierced through his heart with all the time he'd missed with his family— with Zoey.

Had he conveniently forgotten his other life

while in the jungle because of the problems he and Zoey had been having in their marriage? That question knocked the breath from him, leaving him with new doubts. In that moment he didn't know if he could give Zoey what she needed...and deserved.

## Chapter Four

After the waiter cleared away their dinner plates, Zoey relaxed back in her chair and scanned the restaurant, trying to come up with something to say other than pleasantries that had nothing to do with what was wrong between her and Dane. She noticed several other diners glancing their way and shifted in her seat. Obviously the word that her husband had returned from the dead had swept through Sweetwater like a brush fire in an arid climate, as she'd known it would. Not much happened in the town and this was definitely news to her friends and neighbors. She didn't want to be the center of gossip and knew by the tense set to Dane's posture he hated every minute of it.

"It'll be a while before things calm down,"

Zoey offered as an explanation for the man and woman at the next table openly staring at Dane and her while the couple drank their coffee.

"That doesn't mean I have to like it. I feel like I'm under a microscope."

"You are. You're news. The only other exciting thing that has happened lately in Sweetwater was Susan Daniels's house was broken into last week."

The waiter placed a cup of coffee in front of Dane. He quickly picked it up and took a tentative sip, releasing a sigh. "This is good."

Some of his tension abated as he focused on Zoey and his coffee. She tried to do the same, but she felt the stares and wanted to squirm. Like Dane, she didn't like his return being the focal point of Sweetwater's rumor mill.

She dropped her hands to her lap and laced her fingers together—tightly. "What are your immediate plans?"

"Other than getting reacquainted with my family, I have none."

"That doesn't sound like you. You always had everything figured out."

"I've changed."

"Have you?" She heard the doubt in her voice and didn't try to mask it. She'd lived with him for fourteen years and had never seen him change once. He could fixate on a goal with a relentless concentration that had always amazed her. His stubbornness rivaled a mule's.

He laughed, a humorless sound that chilled the air. "My life hasn't been what you'd call normal lately."

"I never thought of your life as normal. Your job wasn't exactly nine-to-five."

He shrugged, took a drink of his coffee and asked, "What's normal?"

"An eight- or nine-hour work day—home in the evenings and on the weekends."

"Well, guess what? You've got me twenty-four seven for the time being."

"The operative words are 'for the time being,' Dane. You and I both know it won't last. You'll go back to your old job and where will that leave us?"

"I don't have answers for you, Zoey." His sharp gaze honed in on her face while he lifted the cup to his lips.

"I won't move back to Dallas. Our life's here now. The family has been disrupted too much in the last few years." There. She had said what she had been feeling, which in the past she had so often kept inside. She'd bowed to the demands of his job, but she couldn't anymore. Her children's—her—well-being was too important to her. Moving would throw the family into turmoil yet again.

He studied the dark contents of his cup. "I could always get transferred to a city nearer here."

"And commute?" She thought of the extra time he would have to travel to his job and wasn't sure that was a solution. In the past his work had demanded long hours.

"Listen, Zoey, I haven't—"

A shadow fell across the white linen tablecloth, and Zoey looked up. Felicia Winters, the town librarian, hovered nearby, adamant interest in her gaze that was trained on Dane. "Felicia, it's nice to see you," she said, hoping to pull the woman's attention away from Dane, whose expression went flat.

The tall woman with not a hair out of place finally glanced at Zoey. "I missed Mandy at story hour this morning."

"Sorry, Blake had a soccer game at the same time." *And my husband appeared unexpectedly on my doorstep last night and threw my life into a tailspin.*

Felicia stuck out her hand toward Dane. "I'm Felicia Winters. I run the library."

Slowly, Dane closed his fingers around hers. "I'm Dane Witherspoon." His tight voice and firmly set mouth conveyed his discomfort.

"Will I see Mandy next week?" Felicia directed the question toward Dane.

Relaxing a little, Zoey answered, "Blake's game isn't until the afternoon so Mandy should be there."

"Good. I know how much Mandy loves to listen to the stories." The woman's stare never left Dane, who narrowed his gaze, his jaw a hard line.

"Thanks for stopping by," Zoey said, hoping the librarian got the message to leave.

But before Felicia parted, she said, "I understand you've been in the Amazon. I wonder if you would come talk to our patrons about the jungle. We have a travelog evening once a month. Someone presents information on a different place each time. We haven't had anyone who can speak knowledgeably on the Amazon."

"I'll think about it," Dane said through gritted teeth.

With a quick nod, the librarian turned away and walked back to her table. The air pulsated with tension.

Without a word Dane tossed his linen napkin on the table, rose and strode toward the maitre d'. When she realized Dane had paid their bill and wasn't coming back to the table, Zoey scrambled for her purse and shawl on the chair next to her. Stares followed her exit, making the hairs on her nape tingle. Outside she found Dane inhaling deep breaths, his hands stuffed into the pockets of his coat.

"Dane, I'm sorry."

He stiffened, his back to her.

"Going out this evening wasn't such a good idea. I should have realized people would be overly interested in your return. This isn't like Dallas."

"You can say that again."

"Felicia loves offering a variety of programs for—"

He spun around and faced her. "I don't want to talk about the Amazon."

"I'll let her know. She means well."

"I grew up in a town a lot like Sweetwater and I left as fast as I could."

She knew he was from Deerfield, Oklahoma, but that was all. She had never gone to his hometown with him since his immediate family was dead and he'd said he had no ties to the place. She'd never pushed him about where he was from; she should have. "Why?" she asked, deciding her usual pattern in the past hadn't worked. She wasn't that same woman.

"Too confining."

"Not enough excitement, people?"

"No, I just never felt comfortable with others sticking their noses in my business."

He wouldn't. He was such a private man, DEA business aside.

When the door behind Zoey opened and a couple exited the restaurant, Dane grabbed her hand and tugged her across the street. The night had cooled since the sun had gone down a few hours before. Halting as she stepped into a park, Zoey draped her shawl around her shoulder.

Dane strolled to a wooden bench not far from the road and sat. Zoey followed, easing down next to him. A huge oak blocked the half moon and a good part of the sky from view. It also threw Dane's features into dark shadows. She suspected that might have been why he had picked this bench to sit on.

He stared at the restaurant entrance as Felicia came out with a gentleman friend. The librarian's voice, accompanied by her laughter, drifted to them, causing Dane to tense.

Finally quiet reigned, only occasionally broken by a trill of a bird or the passing of a car. Dane said nothing for a good ten minutes, and Zoey acknowledged in her heart how wide the gap was between them. She didn't even know what to say to him anymore.

"I will say there's one thing I like about a small town. There aren't as many people out and about on a beautiful Saturday night."

"Sweetwater retires early."

"Does it get up early?"

"Yes, why?"

"I'm thinking of jogging, or at least walking, until I build up my strength to start jogging again."

"And you don't want a lot of people stopping you along the way?"

"It would defeat the purpose of exercising if I had to stop every two feet."

"Then stay away from the lake and this park. It's always busy with joggers and people walking early in the morning."

"Where do you suggest I go?"

"It's not too bad in the neighborhood."

"Do you still jog?"

It had been the one thing they had done together when he was at home in Dallas. A teenager who'd lived next door to them would babysit Blake and

Mandy and they would head to the park not far from their house. "I've been so busy since I moved here that I got out of practice."

"Then why don't you join me? Blake's old enough to watch Mandy and Tara while we walk in the neighborhood. You should find time to exercise."

"I know. I guess I can."

"Good. Then we can start tomorrow morning."

"Tomorrow's Sunday. We go to church at eight-thirty."

He didn't say anything for a moment, and Zoey wished she could see his face. In Dallas they hadn't gone to church much. Usually if she did, it was with the children only. But since coming back to Sweetwater she had rediscovered how important the Lord was in her life. Without His support she wasn't sure she would ever have pulled her life together after Dane's disappearance.

"Then we'll walk at six. You'll have plenty of time to get ready."

"But not you?"

Again Dane went quiet, something Zoey was used to when her husband retreated into himself.

"Dane, come to church with me and the children."

"How can there be a God when there is so much ugliness in the world?"

The question hung in the air between them, heightening the already tall barrier keeping them apart. "But there's so much beauty, too."

"That's a cop-out."

"No, it isn't. It's the truth. The ugliness tests us. We have choices we can make. God didn't guarantee us a paradise on earth. Only one in Heaven."

"Then the human race isn't doing too well."

She'd always known Dane was cynical because of his job, but his cynicism had grown since he had been away. What had happened on his last assignment, which had taken him away from home for six weeks? What had happened in the jungle? "We make mistakes. We're not perfect. Jesus doesn't expect us to be perfect. That's why He died for our sins. We keep trying and learn from those mistakes, but we will make more mistakes."

Dane rose, his back to her. "We'd better get home. I don't want your mom to send out the posse."

"It's only nine. We go to bed early in Sweetwater, but I don't think Mom would be too concerned before at least nine-thirty."

Chuckling, he presented his hand to her.

She fit hers within his grasp, and he pulled her to her feet. She came up against him, so near she could smell the soap he'd used when he'd showered, the mint flavor of the toothpaste he'd brushed his teeth with. Too close. Quickly she stepped away, the back of her legs hitting the edge of the bench. Their clasp disconnected, his arm falling to his side. He stood staring at her for a long moment, his face again in the shadows. Zoey's mouth went dry, her heart pounding against her chest.

"Will Blake still be up when we get home?" Dane asked, starting for the car in the parking lot next to the restaurant.

For a few seconds she watched him striding away, not sure she had the emotional energy to break through the demons that haunted her husband. *Lord, help me. What do I do?*

Dane stopped at the street and waited for her. She hurried toward him, wishing she had an answer to her prayer.

"We'll need to tell Blake our plans to walk tomorrow morning," Dane said as they crossed the street.

"He probably will be up. I'll say something to him."

He paused at the passenger's door of the car.

"But I shouldn't? After the soccer game, he wouldn't even talk to me. He ignored my congratulations. We used to be so close."

"And that's part of the problem. I think he's waiting for you to leave again." *Just like I am,* she silently added, understanding where her son's feelings were coming from.

"I'm not going anywhere. I can't even jog yet. The jungle took its toll on my body and it will be a while before I'm fit to do much of anything."

*Then what happens?* she wanted to ask him yet again. She bit the inside of her cheek to keep the question unasked. Like Blake, she was just waiting for Dane to leave on another DEA assignment and be gone for weeks on end—possibly never come back home. He might have changed in the past two-and-a-half years, but she didn't think he had changed that much. Before his whole life had revolved around his work, around ridding the world of drugs. He would be lost without it. Once he had regained his health, he *would* be gone.

Zoey dunked the herbal tea bag into the hot water, then added a spoonful of sugar and stirred. With a glance at the kitchen wall clock, she winced at the time. Four in the morning. Exhausted but unable to sleep, she made her way to the deck and sank onto a cushioned chair to enjoy the cool spring night, the star-studded sky and the quiet serenade of the insects.

Cupping the mug in her hands, she brought it to her mouth and took several sips of the soothing brew. Blake had been awake, watching television with her mother when they had arrived home. One look at Dane, though, had sent her son upstairs to his room where he'd become absorbed in a book about space travel. As Blake had stomped out of the den, the expression on Dane's face had pained her as much as if she had been the one rejected by their son.

"Lord, I need some help down here. I'm not doing too well on my own." She drank some more of her tea and waited for some kind of divine intervention.

Nothing but the sounds of crickets and birds filled the night. She finished her tea, no longer warm, and started to go inside to fix another cup. She would be up the rest of the night and needed fortification.

A moan penetrated the quiet.

She paused in rising and looked around. Another moan spliced the air. Her gaze riveted to the slightly opened window of the den.

"No! Don't! Get away!"

Her husband's pleading voice shuddered down her length. *Dane's in trouble!* She rushed into the house and ran toward the den. When she burst into the room and flipped on the light, she finally realized how foolish it was not to have thought out her rescue plan. Thankfully he was alone, wrestling with the sheets on his bed, not some thug. The sudden brightness bolted him upright, his eyes wide, sweat dripping off him. For a long moment he stared at her, not really seeing her in the doorway.

Then recognition dawned in his gaze, followed quickly by the circumstances that must have brought her into the room. He took the edge of the sheet and wiped off his face and neck, affording him time to neutralize his expression.

"Sorry, if I woke you," he muttered, not looking at her.

"You didn't. I was having some tea out on the deck. Are you all right?"

"What time is it?" He checked the digital clock on the desk across the room. "It's after four. What are you doing up so early?"

"I couldn't sleep and you aren't going to change the subject. Are you all right? You sounded like you were fighting off an army."

"And you came charging in here armed with what?"

She grinned. She glanced down at her hand that still held the empty mug and lifted it. "This."

Dane combed his fingers through his damp hair. "I'm comforted to know that you're deadly with a mug."

"There you go again changing the subject. What went on in here?"

"Isn't it obvious? I was having a nightmare."

Nothing about her husband was obvious. She walked to the bed and sat. "Care to tell me about it?" Her lungs seized her breath and held it tight until her chest burned.

The sigh that escaped his pursed lips sounded loud in the silence. "I got the thrill of experiencing nearly being burned alive all over again."

"Have you had this nightmare often?" She remembered his cry and wondered if there was more to the dream than he was telling her.

His shoulders lifted in a shrug, but the taut set of them when they settled wasn't casual. "If I'm lucky, only once or twice a week."

"And if you aren't?"

"Almost every night."

His clipped answer sliced through the stillness. A scowl slashed his eyebrows downward, prompting Zoey to reach toward him and brush her fingertips along his hard jaw. "Tell me about the nightmare."

He yanked away from her touch and shot to his feet. "I'd rather not relive it yet again tonight. Once is enough." He headed for the door. "I'm thinking a whole pot of coffee sounds good about now."

"Not to a tea drinker," she said to his retreating back.

He disappeared into the hallway. The stiff line of her body collapsed. Her gaze swept over the rumbled sheets on the bed, the bottom one having come loose in her husband's struggle. Rising, she remade the sleeper sofa, her hands trembling as she tucked the linen beneath the mattress.

He wasn't going to let her in. The urge to scream inundated her, and she fisted the top sheet in her hand until pain forced her to release her grip. The linen floated to the bed.

*So what are you going to do about it?* an inner voice asked.

*Fight for my marriage?*

What choice did she have? Dane was her husband. She'd loved him once so much— that feeling had never really died when she had thought he had—and wanted to be a part of his life.

She squared her shoulders and walked toward the hallway. Then fight she would.

In the kitchen she watched him move about the room, looking in cabinets to locate the items he needed. This brought forward a memory of a time in Dallas not long after Mandy had been born when he'd been trying to be domestic and help out while she was recovering from having their daughter. She'd found him doing the same thing, opening and closing drawers and cabinets, searching for what he needed to use. Except back then, he should have been more familiar with the kitchen. The fact he hadn't been only underscored how little he'd participated in their family life.

"Can I help?" she asked from the doorway.

He paused, glanced up from rummaging in a drawer and said, "Nope. I've got to learn where everything is. I want to pull my own weight around here."

With her shoulder cushioned against the door frame, she folded her arms and tilted her head. "What do you have in mind?"

"Maybe I could do the laundry or learn to cook some of the meals, especially since you're working as a counselor at the high school." He finished getting the supplies—his new coffeepot, the special blend he'd bought, a scooper and a mug. As he measured the granules, he continued, "I know I'm supposed to be getting my strength back and taking things easy, but I've never been one to sit around and not do anything."

"You could always get to know your family."

His movements halted for a few seconds, as though he'd been flash frozen, before he resumed making his coffee. When he completed his task, he turned slowly, leaning back against the counter, his hands clutching its edge. "Does that include you?"

She nodded, her throat contracted. She swallowed hard and finally said, "Most definitely if we want this marriage to succeed." *Do you want it to succeed?* she left unasked. "Now more than ever the children need a stable environment," she added, not completely ready to put her heart totally on the line.

The scent of coffee infused the air, almost enticing her to have a cup. The darkness beyond the window behind Dane reminded Zoey of how little sleep she'd gotten since her husband had returned two days ago. With tired, burning eyes she stared at her husband while he took the kettle from the stove and filled it with water. He set it on the burner and then opened the cabinet where she kept her assortment of teas.

"What would you like to drink? I figure we might as well start our day. It'll be five soon."

Stunned by his gesture—he had never prepared her tea before—she didn't say anything for a moment. Finally because he was waiting patiently for her to answer him, she murmured, "I'd like my English Breakfast tea. That's usually what I drink in the morning."

The whistle on the kettle blasted a shrill sound, and Dane quickly removed it from the burner. After he filled a mug for her, he dunked the tea bag into the hot water. "You used to take one teaspoon of sugar."

She moved toward the refrigerator. "I still do, but I also put half and half in, too."

He slid her mug along the counter toward her. "That's new."

She busied herself stirring her tea, thinking of all the new things in her life. Since his disappearance there had been a series of changes one after another. She wasn't the same person he'd married fourteen years ago. Would he love the woman she had become?

With his mug in hand, Dane made his way to

the table and sat. Zoey was different, more self-assured. He was also different from the man who'd left her to go on an assignment that lasted longer than it was supposed to. There were still gaps in his memory, but he did know one thing: he *had* changed. He wasn't the same man he was two-and-a-half years ago. Could they find the love they had once had for each other? Or had they changed too much, destroying any chance to make this marriage work?

"I know you didn't go to church much when we lived in Dallas, but why don't you come with us this morning?" Zoey took the chair across from him and blew on the hot liquid in her cup. She'd realized she'd already asked him once that night, but she knew it was a good place to begin his healing if he would let God into his life.

He remembered Felicia Winters, the soccer game and all the people—all the questions—and didn't think he was ready. There was no way the parishioners at Zoey's church would let him quietly come to the service and not want to know every detail of what happened for those years he was gone. "Not this week."

"Does that mean you will one Sunday?"

"No" hovered on his lips, but he didn't want to disappoint Zoey yet again. "Maybe."

"Good, because both Mandy and especially Blake are very involved in the church. It would be a wonderful way to get to know them."

"Resorting to blackmail?" He sipped at his coffee, observing a play of emotions flit across her face. Confusion finally won out over anger.

"Blackmail? I'll never resort to blackmail to get someone to come to church. You can't force someone to believe in God. That doesn't mean I won't try to educate, but never blackmail."

He tilted his head toward her. "Sorry, my mistake. I'm glad the children are involved."

"You are?"

He snared her with his gaze. "Yes, Zoey. Your faith is important to you, and I want our children to know about the Lord. It isn't that I don't believe. I just don't see where He's the answer for everything. He certainly wasn't there for me in the jungle."

After taking a large sip of her drink, she put her mug on the table. "So you think He needs to be everywhere making everything wonderful and blissful for everyone."

He winced at her emphasis on *every*. "Shouldn't He?"

"This from the man who prides himself on

being independent? God has given us a brain to think with. We have choices we can make. He isn't orchestrating every movement of our life." She leaned toward him, her expression intense. "But He is there for us when we are hurting and need guidance. He's like a parent. He loves us and helps us, but as we have to with our children, He lets us make our own decisions and face the consequences when we make a mistake. We can't live our children's lives for them because they will grow up and move out on their own."

Silence descended. Dane gulped down the last swig of coffee and thought over Zoey's words. It made sense. He even wished he had the kind of faith she did, but he couldn't see turning his life over to anyone. *He* was the one who had finally left the jungle. *He* was the one who would have to put his life back together. *He* was the one who would have to remember why the plane had crashed in the first place.

"Mommy, I can't sleep," Mandy said, shuffling across the kitchen with Mrs. Giggles in one arm while she rubbed the sleep from her eyes. "Can I stay up with ya and Daddy?"

Mandy stopped by his chair. Dane scooted it

back and patted his lap. "Sure, princess. It's nearly time to get up anyway."

Mandy climbed up and sat with her doll cradled against her. She used his chest as a cushion for her head while she fought a huge yawn. "Good. I had a bad dream."

"Oh," Dane murmured, thinking back to his own. He could almost feel the heat of the fire. He could almost smell the smoke and charred remains of the plane. He trembled, drawing his daughter nearer, hoping she never had to experience a nightmare like that one. "Want to tell me about it?"

"I lost Mrs. Giggles. I looked and looked. Couldn't find her." She yawned again. "I had to make sure she was…okay." Mandy's eyes drifted closed.

Dane looked at Zoey over the top of his daughter's head. "Should I take her back to bed?" he whispered.

Mandy blinked her eyes open and struggled to sit up straight. "No, Daddy. Don't want to lose Mrs. Giggles again."

Zoey listened to her daughter's words, a heaviness pressing down on her chest. So many times dreams were a manifestation of an anxiety. Did Mandy—like her—fear Dane would leave them and become lost again? She had just assumed her daughter would be all right because she seemed so happy to see her father.

"You won't, princess."

Dane's voice caught on his last word. Zoey saw the troubled look in his eyes and knew he was wondering the same thing as she. A person could only mask feelings for so long before they came tumbling out. They were already seeing Blake's. Dread over the months to come encased Zoey in a cold blanket. She was a counselor, used to dealing with people's problems, their emotions, but she didn't know if she could when it was her own family facing turmoil. She realized that was the last few days' exhaustion talking. She didn't have a choice. She would have to deal with it.

Mandy snuggled closer to Dane. "Daddy, Cindy's got a playhouse in her backyard. Can I have one? Then Mrs. Giggles would have her own home."

"Amanda Marie!"

Zoey started to say more when Dane cut in. "I'll see what I can do. That would be a good project for me. Maybe Blake can help me."

Mandy's sleepy expression brightened to a huge grin. "Really?"

Dane glanced at Zoey, a question in his gaze. "If your mother thinks it's okay."

"You've just been manipulated."

"Yeah, I know, but it isn't a bad idea."

"Mommy, what's man—" Mandy's face screwed up in a frown.

"Manipulated is when you get someone to do what you want them to do even if they don't want to."

"But, Daddy does."

Dane chuckled. "She's got you there. What do you think the chances are of me getting Blake to help with the playhouse?"

Hugging Mrs. Giggles tighter to her, Mandy closed her eyes. "Blake loves to build things."

"Good," Dane said with a smile.

"She's right, but…" Zoey let her sentence trail off into silence because she hated to wipe the eagerness from her husband's expression. She had her doubts that Blake would. Her son could be very stubborn—much like his dad.

## Chapter Five

Zoey had needed Samuel's sermon today about going with the flow. She wondered if he had directed it at her. They had talked a few times since Dane had returned and Samuel knew what she was feeling.

Mandy and Blake entered the house first with her taking up the rear. Her empty arms felt strange without Tara in them. But her mother had insisted on taking Tara home with her from church. She'd declared she wanted some alone time with her youngest grandchild.

"What's for lunch?" Blake asked in the middle of the kitchen.

"Sandwiches."

"Peanut butter?" Mandy pulled up the stool so she could reach a top cabinet.

Her daughter's limited list of foods she would eat contained few choices for lunch except peanut butter. *I should take stock out in a company that makes it,* Zoey thought, then said, "Yes. Blake, what do you want? I have the makings of a ham or turkey sandwich."

"Ham." Her son's head jerked around at the sound of a hammer reverberating through the air.

Blake walked toward the back door with Mandy on his heels. Zoey moved to the window over the sink and spied Dane in the backyard, pounding a nail into a two-by-four.

"What's *he* doing?" Blake asked, frowning.

Mandy yanked on the handle, thrusting the door open. "Daddy's started my playhouse!" She rushed out onto the deck, grinning from ear to ear.

The frown on her son's face deepened to a scowl. His teeth dug into his lower lip. "*I* was thinking of making one for Mandy." He spun away from the open door and stalked toward the hallway.

That had been the first time she had heard Blake say he was going to build a playhouse for his little sister. "Why don't you help your dad?"

He halted, his arms stiff at his sides. "If he wants to do it, he can. I don't have the time anyway."

Her son stomped down the hall and up the stairs. Zoey took a deep breath, any peace she'd felt after Samuel's sermon vanishing. *Go with the flow? How can I when the flow is heading toward a waterfall?*

The sound of Mandy giggling drew Zoey's attention. She stepped into the doorway and watched her daughter with Dane, her adoring gaze turned up at him as she listened to what her father had to say.

He looked toward Zoey. His penetrating look jammed a huge knot in her throat as though a fist was stuffed down it. Finally she moved out onto the deck to the railing.

"I'm gonna fix lunch. Would you like a ham, turkey or peanut butter sandwich?"

Mandy tugged on Dane's shirt. "Peanut butter, Daddy. It's the bestest."

He glanced down at his daughter for a few seconds, ruffling her hair. "Just peanut butter?"

"Oh, no. We have grape or strawberry jelly."

"Which do you suggest I have with my peanut butter?"

Mandy cocked her head, her forefinger tapping against her chin. "Well, I had grape yesterday. I think strawberry."

With a twinkle in his eyes, Dane peered

toward Zoey. "Peanut butter and strawberry for the both of us. We'll eat out here if that's all right with you."

"We're gonna have a picnic!" Her daughter jumped up and down, clapping her hands.

"First, Mandy, you need to change out of your good dress."

"Ah, Mommy, I won't get dirty," the five-year-old said as she picked up a piece of wood too big for her and had to settle it against her dress to help her hold it.

Zoey cringed at the streak of dirt she saw on the yellow fabric. "Now, Mandy."

Her daughter dropped the board and slumped toward the steps. "I'll be back."

Dane tossed down the hammer and sauntered toward Zoey. "Sorry about that."

"That's okay. It'll wash clean. Mandy's clothes have to or I'd be in debt buying her new ones all the time."

"Do you need any help making the sandwiches?"

Surprised by the offer, she shook her head. "Nah, I can handle it." Her gaze fell on the lumber stacked behind Dane. "I didn't realize you were gonna start today building the playhouse."

"After you left for church, I stared at the four

walls for half an hour, then decided to do something. So I walked to the super center. I saw Alex Stone there with his pickup and he offered to transport what I needed back here."

"I wondered why Alex was late for church."

"So he goes to the same church as you do?"

"Yeah, I see quite a bit of him since he's also the principal at the high school."

"He told me. The whole way back here he spoke your praises. You've obviously single-handedly reorganized the counseling office."

The heat of a blush scored her cheeks. "I wouldn't say that."

"Well, Alex Stone did."

For a moment Zoey studied the closed expression on Dane's face and wondered about the slight edge to his voice. Was he jealous? That, too, surprised her. "You know my knack for organization. I don't like clutter."

He chuckled, any tension gone between them. "Yes, I know. I still remember that time you cleaned out my closet and threw away my favorite ball cap."

"Oh, please. That old thing was threadbare," she said, her own laughter bubbling up within her as she recalled his shocked expression when he had discovered the neat closet minus his ball cap, which he never wore but had declared was his lucky one. "I'd better go fix lunch before you drudge up some other faulty memory."

"Faulty!" he declared as she quickly escaped into the house.

Mandy raced through the kitchen not five minutes later, banging the door behind her as she went outside. Zoey jumped, splaying her hand over her heart and inhaling deeply. With a glance she spied Mandy helping Dane hammer a board to another one. Satisfied that her daughter was dressed in old jeans and a T-shirt, she finished preparing the sandwiches then went in search of her son.

The door to his bedroom was closed. She rapped on it and waited for him to tell her to come in. No sense provoking him more than he already had been.

"Lunch is ready downstairs."

"Can I eat up here?"

"No, you know you can't eat in your room." She turned to leave, paused and added, "We'll be outside having lunch." She quietly shut his door, her hand lingering on the knob.

*Oh, baby, I wish I could ease your pain,* she thought, heading toward the kitchen after making a brief stop at the linen closet for a blanket.

With a blanket over her arm, Zoey carried a tray laden with their sandwiches and lemonades outside and down the steps to the area where Dane and Mandy were working on the playhouse, at the back of the yard along the fence. "Ready to eat?"

With her tongue sticking out of the side of her mouth and total concentration lining her face, Mandy pounded the hammer into the nail one final time. Leaping to her feet, she pointed to the beginning of a playhouse frame. "Look what I did, Mommy."

"You did good, honey. Let's break for lunch." Zoey gave Dane the blanket to spread over the grass while she held the tray.

Mandy sat cross-legged. "Mrs. Giggles is gonna have a home in no time."

Dane sank down next to his daughter and reached for his peanut butter sandwich. "It may take a few weeks. I haven't built anything in ages. And I want to make sure it'll withstand a windstorm."

"Daddy, ya can do it."

Dane beamed as he took a bite of his food, then washed it down with a swig of lemonade. "Thanks for the vote of confidence."

"Con—vi—dense?" Mandy, with peanut butter smeared on her cheek, looked up at her father.

"Confidence means you're sure I can do it."

"You're my daddy. Ya can." Mandy stuffed a third of the sandwich into her mouth.

Zoey handed her a napkin, indicating she wipe her face. The exchange between father and daughter made her chest expand with conflicting emotions—regret that Dane missed so much time with Mandy and happiness that her daughter had a father again.

"Where's Blake?" Mandy asked after cleaning the red smear off her face.

"He's in his room." Zoey's gaze sought Dane's.

"Why's he spendin' so much time there?"

Mandy's question erased the smile in Dane's eyes. Regret darkened his expression and ripped through Zoey's defenses. None of this was easy, but especially for Dane, she realized, wanting to smooth his concern and pain away.

"Sometimes people like to spend time by themselves," she finally answered her daughter as Dane's impregnable mask fell into place.

"We'll get this done faster with his help." Mandy downed the last of her lemonade, jumped to her feet and hurried back to the stack of boards.

"Mandy, wait for me," Dane called out.

The five-year-old whirled around, trying to snap her fingers and not quite succeeding. "I know. I'll get Mrs. Giggles to help." She ran toward the back door.

"You probably have about three minutes to finish your lunch before she's back."

"Does she ever slow down?"

"When she's asleep."

"That's what I was afraid of." Dane put half of his sandwich back on the tray.

"If you don't want peanut butter, I can fix you something else."

"No—" he shook his head "—no, I'm still not used to eating a lot at one time." One corner of his mouth curved upward. "I'm sure that will change in time, especially with your home cooking."

His compliment, one he had given her many times in the past, brought forth memories of meals spent with the whole family at the table. They had been rare and cherished when they had occurred. So often Dane had been gone or had come home too late to eat with the children. Tears misted her eyes as they took him in.

The back door slammed closed, startling Zoey even though she'd known her daughter was coming back. But she had been so focused on Dane the rest of the world had faded. She averted her gaze and busied herself cleaning up.

Mandy raced to them and settled Mrs. Giggles on the ground under the big oak tree, facing the area where the playhouse was. "I told her we're doin' this for her. Ready, Daddy?"

Dane drank the last of his lemonade then pushed to his feet. "You're a slave driver, but I'm ready to go back to work."

Mandy giggled as she picked up the hammer. Zoey watched the pair for a few minutes, noting Dane's patience with his daughter. It caused the tears to return. So much time lost for both of them.

The hairs on her neck prickled. She glanced over her shoulder and saw Blake standing at the back door watching them through the glass. He turned away when she looked, but she'd seen the longing in her son's expression. A tear slipped down her cheek, and she swiped it away before Mandy glimpsed it and asked a thousand questions she wasn't prepared to answer.

After gathering up the lunch items and stacking them on the tray, Zoey made her way inside, hoping that Blake was still in the kitchen. Her son sat at the table, eating his sandwich, his head bowed. She busied herself rinsing off the dishes and putting them in the dishwasher.

When Blake brought her his plate and glass, she said, "They could sure use your help out there."

"I've got homework."

"Homework! This is a first. You never volunteer to do it." She forced a lightness into her voice, wanting to tease her son into a good mood.

"Well, things change."

He hurried from the kitchen before she could say anything else. Her son had summed up what was happening in the Witherspoon household very well. Right now she would have to settle for her daughters getting to know their father. Hopefully in time, Blake would follow suit. If not—she refused to think about what would happen to the family if her son didn't.

After cleaning up the lunch dishes, Zoey retraced her steps back outside to see what she could do to help. Her daughter's laughter lightened her heart after her encounter with her son.

Mandy saw her and ran up to her. "I'm gonna have a kitchen like ya!"

"Just how big is this gonna be?"

Her daughter drew herself up tall, her shoulders thrust back. "Big enough for me and Mrs. Giggles." She threw her arms around Zoey. "I'm the most luckiest girl there is."

Dane's gaze connected with Zoey's. With Mandy pressed against her, she stared at him, a slow smile entering her eyes and spreading to encompass her whole face. Good. When she'd first come out here a minute ago, she'd worn a worried expression. He was pretty sure why. Blake wouldn't join them. He'd observed him standing at the back door earlier and had hoped he would. But his son had seen him looking and had turned away.

Dane picked up another long board from the stack and laid it on the ground to be nailed. Somehow he had to reach his son. Blake was hurting and he was the reason for it. He couldn't lose his son as he had his younger brother.

"Where's my helper?" he asked, determined not to journey into the past, a past he couldn't change but was resolved not to repeat.

"Here!" Mandy rushed toward him, hopping the last few steps.

"We have a couple of more nails to hammer then we'll be through with this part of the frame. Ready?"

"Yes!" Mandy knelt on the grass.

Dane passed the hammer to her, then held the nail to get her started.

"You're mighty brave," Zoey said behind him.

"No, Mandy's very good. She's got this hammering down."

"Yeah, Mommy. I only hit Daddy's thumb once."

"Ouch!" Zoey's laughter floated to him.

"Not too hard. It has only swollen up twice as big."

"Oh, Daddy, you're too funny."

"Tell me, princess. I've been wondering why you call your doll Mrs. Giggles."

Mandy finished with the first nail. "When I tickle her, she giggles."

"Oh, like this." Dane reached over and tickled Mandy in the side.

His daughter laughed, then launched herself at him, doing the same to him. As they wrestled on the ground, he let her get the best of him. She ended up sitting on his chest until he called out, "Uncle."

Mandy jumped up, brushing her hands together. "I won."

From his prone position on the ground he saw Blake in his bedroom window watching them. The second Dane's gaze touched him, his son darted back behind the curtain. Dane sat up. Blake's continual interest in what they were doing gave him hope. So much of his life was in limbo. He didn't want his family to be. Somehow he had to reconnect with Blake— and with Zoey.

"What are you doing here so late?" Beth Morgan asked from the doorway of Zoey's office at school Wednesday afternoon.

She glanced up from the file she was reading and smiled. "The same thing you are, working. With Dane at the house I've had a chance to catch up on some paperwork."

"Mmm." Her good friend lounged against the jamb, studying her. "Are you sure you aren't just avoiding going home?"

Zoey straightened, restacking the files in front of her. "No. I really have work to do."

Beth came into the office and settled in the chair in front of her desk. "We always have work to do."

Putting her elbow on a pile of papers, Zoey cupped her chin in her hand. "Do you want me to admit I don't want to go home and deal—" She couldn't voice all the seesawing emotions she was experiencing with Dane in the house. One minute she would be happy, the next sad. Then she would become worried, which would evolve into anger.

"And deal with your husband returning from the dead?"

"Exactly." Zoey sighed. "I'm happy he's alive. I'm glad the children are getting to know him all over again."

"But?"

"But I don't know what to feel about him. And Blake is so openly angry at his father. I've tried to get my son to talk to me about it, but he won't say anything. Do you know the past few nights he has gone directly to his room after dinner and done his homework? My son, who never does any unless I threaten him with grounding. I even caught him in bed studying for a test."

Beth leaned forward clasping her hands together. "That's a good thing, Zoey. We want our children to do their homework and study for their tests."

"Yes, but not hide out in their bedrooms."

"Do you want Samuel to try talking to Blake?"

"Yes, please. Samuel has such a way with children. He might be able to find out what's going on in my son's head."

Beth rose. "Sure, I'll say something to my husband tonight. I know some of the kids are going to be working at the church this weekend, cleaning up the flower beds now that spring has sprung."

Zoey put the files away. "I'll walk out with you. You're right. I need to get home."

"It looks like Blake isn't the only one hiding out. You know that won't solve your problems."

While retrieving her purse from the bottom drawer, Zoey slanted a look toward her friend at the door. "Samuel's wisdom is rubbing off on you."

"I think I've been insulted."

Zoey laughed as she switched off the overhead light and locked her office door. "No, I'm complimenting your husband."

The sound of their heels on the tile floor echoed through the hallway as they walked toward the front door. The warm air caressed Zoey when she stepped outside, the light breeze playing with strands of her hair. She brushed some behind her ear.

"This weekend is going be a busy one. Blake has a soccer game before he helps at the church, cleaning up the ground, then he's going to a sleepover at Nate's. I promised Mandy I would take her to the story hour at the library, then she needs some new clothes. She's growing up so fast."

"You don't have to do it all alone anymore. Have Dane help you."

Beth's suggestion caused Zoey to stop in the middle of the parking lot. "You're right. I'd forgotten he could do some of the running around." *At least until he starts working again and is gone all the time,* she added silently.

"See, problem solved just like that." Beth snapped her fingers.

"I wish they all were that easy."

"Have faith, Zoey. Things will work out in time. Look at Samuel and me. Never thought I wanted a second family and I wouldn't change places with anyone in this world. How did I think traveling would ever take the place of family?"

"Tell that to my husband. But in his case it's his job." Zoey began walking toward her minivan.

"Maybe he's changed since being away."

Changed? Zoey didn't think so. She pictured his closed expression and the strained periods of silence when he wouldn't let her in. That was the Dane who had disappeared on a mission in South America. "See you tomorrow."

On the short drive to her house Zoey thought of Beth and her circle of friends. They had helped eased the pain of mourning Dane's death when she had first arrived in Sweetwater two years ago, with a brand-new baby and barely holding her life together. She still depended on them for advice and guidance.

The gray dimness of dusk invaded the landscape as she pulled up into her driveway and parked. One day she needed to clean out the garage enough to get her van into it, she mused while heading for the front porch of the home she'd lived in when she was a child. Her mother had insisted on getting a small house for herself while she and the children lived here. Zoey was comforted by familiar surroundings, but the house was old and needed some work on it.

*When am I gonna have the time?* she asked herself, inserting the key into the lock.

*Dane is here now. He can help.* Again she was reminded she wasn't alone any longer. But she couldn't shake the feeling it felt as if she were alone.

When she opened the front door, the quiet of house greeted her. Where was everyone? "Hello!"

Silence.

Then she heard the laughter coming from the backyard. She walked through the empty kitchen and out onto the deck, finding Mandy, Tara and Dane near the partially built playhouse. Her youngest daughter sat on the grass, rubbing her eyes while Mandy put some of the tools away.

Her oldest daughter saw her. "Mommy, you're home!"

Dane glanced up from stacking some wood to the side of the framed structure. "We lost track of time. Didn't realize it was getting so late."

Zoey made a beeline for Tara, seeing her crunching up her face into a frown that was a prelude to her cry. She snatched up the toddler into her arms. "It's okay, baby." As Tara's cry erupted, Zoey felt her daughter's forehead. Heat grazed her fingertips. "She's hot."

Dane dropped the last piece of scrap wood. "What?"

"She's got a fever."

Hurrying to her, he laid his hand over Tara's brow. "When she got up from her nap a few hours ago, she was fussy, didn't want me to hold her. But when I brought her out here, so Mandy and I could work on the playhouse, she calmed down."

Zoey walked toward the back door. "She's never fussy after her nap unless something's wrong."

The tight edge to his wife's voice conveyed her anger, as did the firm set to her mouth. Dane watched her disappear inside, feeling her censure as if she had spoken it out loud. She'd made it plain he should have known that Tara was coming down with a fever.

Mandy tugged on his shirt. "Is Tara okay?"

"Yeah, princess. I'm sure she is. She's just not feeling well." He hoped he was right. This incident underscored how little he knew about his own children—even Blake, whom he would have said he knew very well at one time. But not anymore. His son was a stranger to him and he was at a loss how to get through to him. "We'd better go inside. It's getting dark."

Mandy took his hand as they approached the steps to the deck. "I'm hungry. What's for dinner?"

Dinner? He should have planned something. Zoey had told him she was going to work late at school, and yet he had gotten so wrapped up in the playhouse, he'd forgotten all about dinner. "How about pizza?"

"Yes! I want cheese pizza."

"Okay. Do you know what Blake and your mother like?"

She exaggerated a shrug, cocking her head to the side.

"I guess I'd better ask them then." Dane

opened the door to the kitchen and entered, flipping on the light as night fell.

Mandy ran ahead and darted down the hallway to the den. Dane heard the television come on as he climbed the stairs to the second floor. Tara's cries resounded through the house, making a mockery of his good intentions.

He found Zoey in his youngest daughter's bedroom, rocking her. She didn't look toward him when he came inside, but he could tell she knew he was there by the stiffening of her body.

"I'm ordering something to eat. I thought pizza. What kind do you like?"

"Canadian bacon."

"How about Blake?"

"The same."

"Will she be all right?" Helplessness swamped him as Tara squirmed and whined, not happy with any position she was held in.

"I hope so."

"I'll order the pizza, then come back and take over. You haven't had a chance to get comfortable since coming home."

"That's okay. I'm used to this."

Zoey's expression forbade further discussion. Dane backed out of the room and went downstairs to find the telephone book. After placing the pizza order, he checked on Mandy to make sure she was all right, then set out the dishes for their takeout dinner. When he was finished, he stood in the kitchen, wondering what he should do next.

For a few seconds he thought of going back to Tara's room and forcing the issue with Zoey. No, he didn't know his youngest daughter's habits yet, but that didn't mean he had neglected her. The last time he had changed Tara's diaper, an hour before Zoey had come home from school, his daughter hadn't been feverish.

He started for the stairs again when he saw Zoey at the top of them. Their gazes linked, the tired lines of her face gripping him in a viselike hold. She descended the steps, breaking visual contact with him. Her slow pace, her grasp on the banister, emphasized her exhaustion.

"I'm sorry I disappointed you," he said, blocking her path at the bottom of the stairs.

"I'm not disappointed, Dane."

"Then what are you?"

"That's a good question. I don't know what I feel right now. I haven't slept well since your return and it's catching up with me."

"Then go to bed after dinner. I can make sure Mandy and Blake get to bed and check in on Tara. Is she asleep?"

"Yes."

He reached out and took her arm. "Look, I know I haven't been around, but I'm here now. Let me help you."

She released a long, deep breath. "I don't think I have a choice. I hope the pizza gets here—"

The doorbell rang, cutting off Zoey's last words.

Dane hurried to answer it. After paying for the two large pizzas, he called Mandy to dinner, gave the boxes to Zoey and took the stairs to get Blake. Nearing his son's bedroom, he thought of the times he had faced down criminals and realized he was more anxious now than then. In the past he had known what to do in those type of situations, but he didn't have the slightest idea what to do to get through to his son.

He knocked on his door and waited until Blake said, "Come in." The surprised look on his son's face made it obvious he'd been expecting Zoey. That look quickly evolved into a scowl.

"Dinner's ready. We're having pizza." Dane turned to leave, then stopped and glanced back at his son. "I sure could use your help with the playhouse. Mandy's great but some things take two guys."

He didn't expect Blake to say anything and

his son didn't disappoint him. His continued frown was the last thing Dane saw as he closed the door. He went by Tara's room and peeked in to make sure she was still sleeping. Walking softly to her crib, he peered down at his youngest child. Love inundated him. He hadn't known about her until recently and already he couldn't imagine his life without her.

Tara's cheeks were flushed. Moving, she whimpered, her eyes still closed. Dane started to stroke her, hoping to soothe her, but before he had a chance, she settled down, sticking her thumb into her mouth and sucking on it, just like Mandy had at that age. The memory was bittersweet.

After a hot bath Zoey dressed for bed, then walked down the hall to see how Tara was before she went to sleep. When she eased open the door, she discovered Dane sitting in the rocking chair in the dark. He looked toward her but didn't say anything. She tiptoed to the crib, checked on Tara, then turned toward her husband.

"You don't have to stay in here," she whispered, realizing she had been unfair to him earlier. That had been her exhaustion and wariness talking.

"I know." He unfolded his long length from the chair and stood. He followed her to the door. In the hallway, he continued, "I need to get Mandy ready for bed anyway. Good night."

He turned away. She stopped him with her hand on his arm. "I'm the one who should be sorry. Tara's been having trouble with her ears for the past six months. This could be another ear infection. There was no way you would know that." She released her hold on him. "If she isn't better tomorrow morning, I'll have to take her to the doctor."

"I can if you need to go to work."

"No!"

Dane stepped back.

"I mean, I will do it," Zoey said.

"She's my daughter, too."

"Yes, but—" How could she tell him she was afraid to surrender too much to him? What would happen when he left again? She couldn't become dependent on him. "You haven't driven the van yet," she offered as an inane excuse.

"I still remember how to drive and my license is still valid. I haven't really had a need to. That doesn't mean I can't." He curled his hands into fists, his lean features pulled into a somber expression.

Too weary to think beyond going to bed, she said, "We'll discuss it tomorrow morning." She pivoted and walked toward her bedroom.

The second her head hit the pillow and she closed her eyes, sleep descended quickly like the setting sun in the tropics.

Someone shook her shoulder. She didn't want to get up. The black void beckoned.

"Zoey, get up! It's Tara. She's burning up."

## Chapter Six

Zoey shot up straight, her heart pounding. "Where is she?"

Dane switched on the lamp next to her bed. "Right here."

She took her child into her arms, feeling the heat emanating off her. Tara's lethargic state with the occasional whimper alarmed Zoey. She scrambled off the bed, still cradling her youngest to her chest. "I'd better take her temperature."

"Where's the thermometer?"

"In my bathroom. In the cabinet."

As Dane left, Zoey smoothed Tara's hair from her forehead and rocked her in her arms, cooing to her. A minute later Dane was back, thrusting the thermometer into her hand. Zoey took it and stuck it into her daughter's ear. The thermometer registered one hundred five. The beating of her heart accelerated, a film of perspiration coating her face as she fought her panic. None of her children had ever had a temperature spike that high.

"I need to get her to the emergency room," she said in a high-pitched voice that conveyed her fear. She gave Tara to Dane so she could throw on some clothes.

"I'm coming with you."

"No, someone has to stay with Mandy and Blake."

"Call your mother. I'm coming with you."

The firmness in his voice coupled with her worry prompted her to say, "Fine, if she can get here in a few minutes."

Zoey quickly placed a call to her mother, who assured her she would be there immediately. After hanging up, Zoey stepped into her walk-in closet and threw on the nearest sweatshirt and pair of jeans.

When she emerged, dressed, she found Dane cuddling Tara, stroking her back, concern engraved on his features that had to mirror her expression. She glanced at the digital clock on the beside table and noted the late hour—one in the morning.

She took Tara from Dane, needing to hold her daughter, as though she could absorb the heat raging through her child's body. Walking into the hallway, she noticed that Dane was still dressed and said, "Thank goodness you checked on her before going to bed."

"I wasn't going to bed. I fell asleep in the rocking chair and woke up when I slumped to the side. I heard Tara moving around, moaning softly, and I got up to see what was wrong."

"Let's get her in her car seat so when Mom arrives we can leave right away." Zoey retrieved a light blanket from Tara's crib to cover her daughter, then proceeded down the stairs.

As Zoey strapped Tara into her seat, her mother pulled up next to her van and slid out. Zoey clutched the door in relief.

"Don't worry about a thing. I'll take care of the kids." Emma hugged Zoey.

She ran a shaky hand through her hair that she hadn't even bothered to brush. "Thanks, Mom. I don't know how long we'll be, but I'll give you a call when I know something."

Dane came around the van and held out his hand. "I'm driving."

"Are you sure?" Zoey asked, dropping the keys into his palm. He hadn't driven—in fact, had avoided driving—since he had come back five days before.

"Yes." He strode to the driver's side and got in.

"I'll be praying, hon," Emma said, stepping away from the van while Zoey climbed in.

During the ten-minute drive to the hospital, silence ruled. Zoey's thoughts scattered into a hundred different directions. Each time she latched onto a fragment she shoved it away in horror. Illness after illness taunted her the whole way until her breathing was labored and rivulets of sweat rolled down her face even though the spring air was chilly.

At the emergency room Zoey reluctantly handed over Tara to the nurse and doctor on duty, Zoey's whole body trembling by the time she released her daughter. Standing off to the side, she watched as the medical team began to work on Tara. Her legs weak, Zoey clasped Dane. He wound his arm around her, pressing her close to his side and keeping her upright.

*God, help Tara. Please don't let anything bad be wrong. Please let her be all right.*

Zoey said the silent prayer over and over, her gaze never leaving the scene taking place in the emergency room cubicle. And through the whole ordeal, Dane's strength surrounded her.

His steady presence cracked her resistance and planted a seed of hope.

*"They want me back on the job. I'm returning to South America and will be gone for the next six months,"* Dane said, standing in the doorway. *"They need me."*

*"No! We need you! You can't leave again."* Zoey took a step toward her husband, but he backed away.

*With one last look, he turned to leave. She reached out to stop him and her hand clenched the air. He was gone, as if he had never been there in the first place.*

"No!" Zoey jerked awake, catching herself before falling out of the rocking chair in Tara's room.

Bright sunlight leaked through the drawn curtains. Zoey pushed her hair back from her forehead and shook the sleep from her foggy mind. She must have slept for a while. Her muscles protested the uncomfortable position she'd been in and screamed for her to stretch them.

She rose, her legs unsteady. Clutching the back of the chair, she rolled her head around in a full circle, lifting her arms high above her head, as though she could touch the ceiling, then arched her back, curling her shoulders.

Checking the crib, she noticed that Tara was still sound asleep, her chest rising and falling gently. Zoey fingered her child's cheek and breathed easier when she felt coolness against her skin.

She bowed her head and whispered, "Dear Heavenly Father, thank You for healing my daughter. Watch over her and keep her close to You. Please help her to get totally well. And thank You for Dane's presence at my side last night. It was nice not to go through it alone. I've felt so alone for a long time. Thank You, God, for being in my life. Amen."

"Zoey, is Tara all right?"

She spun around, facing Dane, standing in the doorway. Her nightmare came back, seizing her breath. She forced a deep gulp of air that burned as she held it for a few heartbeats too long. "Yes. She's still sleeping. I was praying."

"She scared me last night." He crossed the room.

"Me, too. She's had ear infections before but nothing as bad as that. Thank you for being with me at the hospital." She was tempted to lean against him as she had done in the emergency room while the nurse had given Tara a tepid water bath to help bring her fever down. Light-headed, Zoey swayed toward him but caught herself before she gave in to her impulse. She couldn't get used to Dane's support. Like in her nightmare, he could be gone at any time.

He took her hand. "Come on. You need some rest. I called the school and said you wouldn't be in today."

"I just took a nap."

Dane checked his watch. "Yeah, all of forty minutes. You need to lie down in your bed and really get some sleep."

"But—"

He placed his forefinger over her mouth, stilling her words. "I'll make sure Tara's all right while you sleep. You don't need to worry, Zoey. I'm here." He tugged her toward the door.

*For how long?* her sleep-deprived mind screamed while her lips tingled from his touch, making a mockery of her cynical caution where her husband was concerned.

Out in the hallway Zoey slipped her hand from his, needing to sever any physical contact in order to keep her emotional distance. "You didn't get any more sleep than I did. In fact, you got less, so if anyone should go lie down, it should be you." She was determined to deal with the situation as she had the past few years without him.

A half grin appeared on his face. "Let's make a deal." He covered the space between them, taking both her hands and tugging her toward her bedroom. "If you lie down and take a nap, I will do the same right after you get up. Deal?"

At the doorway into her room she spied her bed, the covers messed up from her interrupted sleep the night before. Their softness beckoned her. Okay, maybe she needed to rest for a little while and would let him watch Tara while she did. That didn't mean she would come to depend on him again, she thought as he drew her forward.

"Don't let me sleep longer than two hours. I'm sure I won't, but wake me up if I do. And if Tara wakes up, she can have some more medication for her fever in an hour and a half."

"I'll take care of everything, Zoey." He gently pushed her down onto the mattress.

When she curled onto her side, he drew the top sheet up to her shoulder, bent down and kissed her on the cheek, then quietly left her alone to deal with her tumultuous feelings. Why did he have to go and kiss her? Why did he have to be so nice and—there for her? Now, after years of not being?

"I appreciated your help today with the team."

"Anytime." Dane took Alex Stone's hand and shook it.

"Be careful what you say. I might take you up on that offer."

Dane looked the man in the eye. "I meant it. I enjoyed helping today." *I need something to do,* he silently added. *Especially if it involves Blake.*

With a glance toward the group of boys all drinking their pop, Alex said, "We practice every Tuesday and Thursday evening here, if the weather is decent. My assistant coach backed out at the last minute and no one has stepped forward."

"Then you've got yourself a new assistant coach."

"Good. Blake can fill you in on our procedures and this league. Like today, our games are usually Saturday. We'll probably go to at least two tournaments, which if we win, our games will take up the whole weekend. These guys are getting serious about their soccer, especially your son."

Dane located Blake in the crowd, his head

tipped back as he downed the last of his pop. "Yes, I could tell. He gives one hundred percent."

"The work you did with the goalie was great. That move you showed him cost the other team a goal. I hope you can continue to help him. Now, let me introduce you to the guys."

Alex walked the few feet to the cluster of boys around the ice cooler, motioning for them to come closer. When he had their attention, he said, "How about a cheer for our new assistant coach, Mr. Witherspoon, who has graciously volunteered his time?"

The whole team rooted for Dane, except his son, who stepped away from the group, his shoulders hunched, his head down, which had become his usual stance of late.

Alex raised his arms to quiet the boys. "From what I understand he's had a lot of experience playing soccer. His last position was goalie so we'll be able to use his expertise. I know how much you all want to win the league this year. Mr. Witherspoon will be here to help us go all the way."

Another cheer went up with the team punching their fists into the air. Again Dane noticed the absence of enthusiasm from his own son even though he lifted his arm as the others did and let out a yell. He'd been in Sweetwater a week and nothing had changed with his son.

The boys began to disperse, grabbing their gear and leaving with their parents. Blake trotted toward his bag, slowly stooped and picked it up, then headed for the minivan, his shoulders still slumped, his head still bowed as though the ground was the most fascinating object he'd ever seen.

Dane scanned the soccer fields, crowded with parents and their children. The sun beamed down, warming the early morning chill. There wasn't a cloud in the sky. A perfect day. Yeah, right! His life was in a shambles. He didn't have any idea what he was going to do beyond today. There were gaps in his memory that ate at him, terrorizing his sleep. His son hated him, didn't want him around. His guilt still plagued him. And his wife was a different person. *He* was a different person.

Wilbur Thompson walked past Dane, tossing a narrowed look at him. "He thinks he's some hotshot DEA agent. My son could outshoot him," he mumbled to the old man next to him.

That was his problem, Dane thought. He *didn't* know who he was anymore and he certainly didn't feel like a DEA agent. And that was part of the problem, since his job had always defined him in the past. With a shake of his head he started for the van. As he drew closer to the vehicle, he noticed his son was in the backseat, the same as when he had ridden with him to the game. Like a chauffeur. That underscored their relationship more than anything else.

As Dane backed out of the parking space and pulled onto the road, he said, "I thought we could grab some hamburgers before we head for church."

Not a word from the backseat. The chill in the van had nothing to do with the outside temperature, which was a pleasant sixty-five.

When Dane stopped to order at the drive-through, Blake finally said, not to Dane but to the invisible person behind the speaker mounted on the sign, "I'll have large fries and a double cheeseburger with a chocolate milkshake."

*Patience, Dane.* He gritted his teeth and drove to the window to pay for their order. After getting the sack with their food, he handed it to Blake, who hurriedly withdrew his food then dropped the bag onto the front seat. Dane's hamburger rolled out onto the floor.

Dane calmly pulled to the curb and threw the

van into Park, then swiveled around to spear his son with his regard. "It's clear things aren't working out between us."

"You think?" Blake muttered, his gaze glued on the window to his side.

"Yes, I think," Dane said in a surprisingly level voice when his impulse was to shake some sense into his son. "You're angry with me so why don't you tell me what's wrong so maybe we can move beyond it? Keeping it inside isn't good." He should know. He was an expert at keeping his feelings inside.

Blake continued to stare out the window with his arms crossed over his chest and his mouth set in a stubborn line.

"Son, I'm here for you. Talk to me."

Nothing.

With a deep sigh, Dane twisted back around and threw the van into Drive. "I'm not going anywhere so you and I need to learn to live peacefully together."

Still nothing.

In the rearview mirror Dane saw his son remain frozen in that defiant position for several blocks before he decided to unwrap his hamburger and take a bite. In the mirror their gazes connected and Blake quickly averted his.

"I wasn't gone because I chose to be gone for two-and-a-half years." The deafening silence spoke volumes to Dane. He didn't know what to do to tear down his son's barriers. "My plane crashed in the jungle and I was injured badly, all out of my control. For a long time I didn't know who I was. I—"

"Why did you volunteer to be the assistant coach? I don't want you to help the team."

The heated force behind his son's words could have melted the polar ice caps. Dane gripped the steering wheel, turning into the parking lot at the church. "Mr. Stone needed someone and I am available."

"Until you leave again," Blake muttered, then snatched up his uneaten lunch and exited the van the second Dane had come to a stop.

His son raced toward the garden at the side of the building where people were gathered. Dane retrieved his hamburger from the floor, grabbed the almost-empty sack and stuffed his food down into it. At a much slower pace Dane made his way toward the group. Seeing a trash can, he tossed his bag, with his untouched meal, into it, his appetite gone like his son.

"Hello. You must be Dane Witherspoon, Zoey's husband. I'm Samuel Morgan. It's good to see you here." The tall man offered him his hand.

After greeting the minister, Dane said, "Can I help? I don't have any plans for the afternoon."

"Sure. We can always use an extra pair of hands."

"Where do you want me?"

"You can help Blake with the flower beds."

Dane thought back to the past fifteen minutes in the van and decided his son needed some cooling-off time. *He* needed some cooling-off time. Forcing himself on Blake probably wasn't the wisest option at the moment. "He's not too happy with me right now."

"Zoey said something to me about talking with Blake."

"She did? She didn't say anything to me." A defensive tone entered his voice that he couldn't conceal.

"Blake's spending the night at our house tonight, and she thought it might be a good time to pull him to the side and see if he would talk about what's bothering him."

There was a part of Dane that wanted to reject Samuel Morgan's help; there was a part that needed his assistance because he certainly wasn't succeeding.

"Where do you need me?" Dane asked again, not wanting to go into his relationship, or lack thereof, with his son.

"I could use some help raking the last of the dead leaves up."

"Fine," Dane replied, leery of Samuel. He'd put his trust in the Lord to help his little brother and Jacob had ended up dead. He couldn't afford to make that kind of mistake again, especially when it involved his son.

After handing Dane a rake, Samuel moved to the area of the garden where all the fallen leaves had gathered, trapped by the stone wall that encircled the Garden of Serenity. Positioning the large trash can between them, Samuel began to rake.

For a few minutes silence punctuated the air, then Samuel broke the quiet with, "Our wives grew up together."

Dane closed his eyes, realizing he wouldn't escape. "They did?"

"Yeah. Beth, my wife, Zoey, Tanya, Darcy and Jesse have this little group that meets most Saturday afternoons at Alice's Cafe."

"What do they meet about?" Dane asked, aware that Zoey had missed last Saturday because of him.

Samuel paused, leaning on his rake. "You know, that's a good question. Beth doesn't tell me much about these meetings. But I do know they are very close. I think Beth looks at the other four as her sisters even though she has several siblings. Maybe that's it. They have some secret sisterhood."

Zoey hadn't said a word to him concerning the others. Again he realized how much he didn't know about his wife. He couldn't have said that three years ago. The gulf between him and Zoey widened even more.

"We should start our own," Samuel said, resuming his work.

"Sisterhood?"

Samuel laughed. "That would get the tongues wagging."

Out of the corner of his eye Dane saw a police car pulling up to the curb by the garden. A large man in a blue uniform climbed out of the vehicle and strode toward a young teenager near his son. Samuel stopped, tossed down his rake and headed for the pair. Dane followed.

"Eddy, I need you to come with me."

"What the problem, Zach?" Samuel stepped in between the two.

"Reverend." The police chief nodded toward

him. "There was another robbery last night and someone saw Eddy running from the scene."

The minister pivoted toward the teenager, one brow arched in question. "Do you know anything about this?"

Eddy threw down his spade, the blade end sticking in the soft ground. "The person must have been mistaken."

"Whether he is or not, we'll have to sort this out down at the station. I've got a call into your dad. He'll meet us down there."

The teenager stomped past the police chief. "Yeah, I bet he will."

"Sorry, Samuel, about this interruption." Zach Thompson hurried after Eddy.

Dane came to stand next to the minister. "Trouble in paradise?"

"You could say that. We've had a rash of robberies lately, and as much as I wish I didn't feel this way, I wouldn't be surprised if Eddy O'Neal knew something about it."

"A troubled teen?"

"Most definitely. I've tried to include him as much as he'll let me in some church activities, but he blames his father for his mother leaving last year. Their relationship isn't what it should be and that's putting it mildly."

Like his and Blake's. The irony of the situation struck Dane and the similarities between his younger brother's and his situation. Was it true that if a person didn't understand history he was doomed to repeat it?

"Have you talked to him, Reverend?" Dane was mildly surprised that he was asking that question, but maybe Zoey was right and Blake—like Eddy—could be helped by an outside source.

"I've tried but the person has to want to listen before it's effective. Eddy isn't ready yet."

"I'm not sure that Blake is ready."

Samuel studied him. "Do you care if I try?"

Suddenly Dane felt exposed for all the world to see, his emotions laid bare. His throat closed. The pressure in his chest built until he wasn't sure he could draw in a decent breath. "Not if it'll help my son."

"I hope I can."

As Samuel returned to his raking, flashes of Dane's past—his desperate battle to save his brother from drugs, his failure to succeed in that goal, the plane as it plunged toward the green canopy, then nothing but a blank slate—tumbled through his mind as though he were rolling down a hill, gaining momentum the farther he went until he crashed at the bottom, as battered and bruised as his emotions felt at the moment. Inhaling then exhaling deep breaths finally alleviated the tightness about his chest.

He scooped up his rake and attacked the pile of leaves, determined to work until exhaustion claimed him. Maybe then the nightmare wouldn't come.

An hour later a three-car caravan came into the parking lot with horns blaring. Everyone stared at the occupants as they piled out of the vehicles with a couple of ice coolers in hand.

"Ah, I see my wife has finally arrived with the goodies," Samuel said beside Dane.

The last person to climb from one of the cars was Zoey. His heart skipped a beat at the sight of her. Her large, soulful eyes pierced his armor as she sashayed toward him with a saucy look. Her long blond ponytail bounced behind her and a mischievous grin dimpled her cheeks.

"So what do we owe this honor to?"

"We've come to rescue y'all," Zoey said in an exaggerated Southern drawl. She waved her hand toward the group of women that accompanied her. "We've brought gifts for the hard workers."

"Gifts?" He peered at the two ice chests sitting on the stone path in the garden.

"Pop and candy."

"My kind of diet."

"I remember your sweet tooth."

"That hasn't changed, I'm quickly realizing. Do you know in a week's time I've gained three pounds?"

"Good." She playfully pinched his side. "You need to. I have a few I could give you."

He started for the cooler. "Do you want anything?"

"Something diet."

"You brought diet for the kids?"

"No, for us." Zoey indicated the other four ladies. "We certainly weren't going to watch you all drink."

Dane snagged two sodas and a chocolate bar, then walked back to Zoey. He noticed Blake wolfing down his drink and candy while standing with several boys about his age. He didn't know the names of a lot of the people and decided in that moment he'd better starting learning who everyone was. He could no longer keep himself separated if he wanted his marriage to work. He'd never gotten involved in a community—never had the time—but maybe that needed to change.

Glancing at Zoey, he saw the animated expression on her face as she said something to one of her women friends. She was involved to the point he didn't know if he could talk her into leaving Sweetwater when he finally made a decision about his future.

"Here." He handed her a diet soda.

"Dane, this is Beth, Samuel's wife, and a good friend."

"Nice to meet you." He shook Beth's hand, liking the warm smile that lit her face. "I understand you work at the high school, too."

"Trying to instill English into ninth and tenth graders."

"Are you succeeding?" Dane took a swig of his drink.

"Some days are better than others. Excuse me. I see Craig going for his third candy bar." Beth made a beeline for a young boy who had been with Blake.

"That's her stepson and one of Blake's friends," Zoey said with a chuckle as she watched Beth firmly remove the chocolate bar from Craig's hand.

"He's not on the soccer team."

"No. But I think they want to start a band together."

"A band! My son?" Again he was reminded of what little he knew of Blake. Once he'd thought he'd known everything about his son. "Why haven't I heard him playing anything?"

"Because Samuel gave them some space in his detached garage to practice."

"What's he play?"

"Keyboard. They haven't really been playing long. Sean sings. Craig and Nate play the guitars."

"What else is going on that I need to know about?"

## Chapter Seven

The regret Zoey heard in Dane's question drew her full attention. If they hadn't been standing out in the middle of the garden next to the church, she would have smoothed the lines of his brow, cradled his face and kissed him. Kissed him!? One wistful expression and she turned to mush, forgetting all those nights—even before his disappearance—spent alone, her arms aching for her husband.

"Blake loves to play soccer and the keyboard. He's active in the youth group and has a nice core group of friends. He hates to clean his room, and if I let him, he would watch TV for hours. His grades are so-so. That about sums him up."

"He doesn't like school? He used to."

"Not for several years."

"Since I disappeared?"

"Yep. In fact, I hired a tutor for one semester right after you...disappeared, because he and I couldn't work together. He wouldn't listen to me."

Pain clouded his eyes. Dane stepped closer, grasping her arm. "I'm so sorry."

This time she did cup his face, compelling him to look deep into her eyes. "You didn't do it on purpose. I know that, and I think one day Blake will, too."

"Do you *really* feel that way?"

"Yes, I feel that way. I won't kid you. I didn't like all the times you were away, but I do know you were doing a job that needed to be done. I know how important the battle against drugs is for you. And I certainly know you didn't plan to stay away for so long."

His eyes closed for a few seconds before his gaze locked with hers, such sorrow in his expression. "I've seen firsthand the destructiveness of drugs."

Before his life had been so involved, she remembered that first year of their marriage Dane had volunteered at a halfway house in Dallas for people who had been on drugs. But for some reason he couldn't deal with that for long and quit, throwing his total energy into being the best DEA agent there was. With his background in counseling, she'd never quite understood why he'd left the halfway house, but he wouldn't talk about it with her.

The pain emanating from him cracked her heart. So much stood between them, but in that moment, for just a split second, nothing did. Then it was gone, Dane severing visual contact, his mask of invincibility in place.

"Thanks for bringing the treats. I didn't eat lunch so this is it till dinner." Dane held up the candy bar, then began unwrapping it.

"Why didn't you?" She put some space between them, achingly conscious of his barriers that had descended. It was so second nature to him to erect those walls around his innermost self that she didn't think she could ever get through, even with her counseling skills.

"It ended up on the floor of the van." Dane finished the last bite of his candy bar, then washed it down with some pop.

"How?"

"Blake."

"Oh, Dane, I'm sorry. Maybe you should have gone with Mandy today."

"No way! Story hour with Felicia Winters? I don't think so."

The lightness that crept into his voice touched a responsive chord in her. "Avoiding her won't stop her from hounding you to do a program on the Amazon."

"I've been trained in evasive tactics. She's no match for me." He tossed his empty can into the trash bag nearby. "Besides, I would have missed the opportunity to volunteer to be the assistant coach for Blake's soccer team."

"Did Alex explain to you why the last one backed out?"

Dane shook his head, wariness creeping into his expression.

"There are several adamant parents on the team who can be quite...persistent. Actually they put Felicia to shame on their hounding abilities."

"How does Alex handle it?"

"He's become quite good at evasive tactics, too. Also, he's learned to tune out those particular parents and their relatives."

"Is one of them Wilbur Thompson?"

"Yes! Has he said something to you already?"

"Not about the coaching. The police chief seems young to have an eleven- or twelve-year-old."

"It's Zach's older brother's son. But Zach is

older than he looks. I have to admit his youth has thrown a few people off."

"This town just gets more interesting by the second."

"So what do you all think?" Dane asked, cleaning off Tara's face before lifting her out of her high chair, his daughter wiggling the whole time to get down.

The second Tara's feet hit the wooden floor she ran toward the door as fast as her little legs could take her. Both Alex and Samuel chuckled, watching Tara escape the kitchen, heading toward the den to join Mandy. After the scare with her ear infection four weeks ago, it was good to see her so active.

"I think it's needed in Sweetwater. A youth center might give some of them, who have too much idle time on their hands, something constructive to do." Alex sipped his iced tea.

"Are you thinking of the rash of break-ins that have occurred lately?" Dane asked, remembering the last one had been several blocks away just five days before.

"I'm not saying Eddy is involved. The police didn't have enough to hold him, but I think he knows something."

"We might be able to get the old building next to the church. It needs fixing up, but it's not being used." Samuel rose and walked to the coffeepot to pour some more into his mug.

"Is it safe?" Alex asked.

"I think so." Samuel sat again at the kitchen table. "Wilbur Thompson owns the property. I can approach him about what you proposed, Dane."

Dane stiffened. "Don't use my name in connection with this youth center. If Wilbur finds out it was my suggestion, he won't let us rent the building." He could still recall his last encounter with the older gentleman who also happened to live at the end of the block. He wasn't too happy with Dane using someone besides his grandson as the goalie and had told him in no uncertain terms to knock it off.

"Speaking of money, where will we get the money to fix the building up, buy some equipment and pay the rent?" Alex's cell phone buzzed. He glanced at the caller ID, then put it back in his pocket. "How uncanny. That's Wilbur's number."

"Calling to complain again about your assistant coach," Dane said with a chuckle.

"No doubt. That's why I'm not in a rush to return the call. No reason to borrow trouble."

"That's Wilbur, trouble with a capital *T*." Dane shifted his gaze from Alex to Samuel. "Do you have any idea where we could get the funding needed to get started?"

"I think the church's outreach program could get the ball rolling. And Nick's been looking for a worthy cause to contribute to. I bet I can convince him this is one. His children will be teens soon enough."

The back door opened, and Zoey came into the house with Blake trailing behind her. His son saw Dane and frowned, his eldest child's usual expression when in his presence. Blake's gaze slid to each man at the table, then he hurried through the kitchen and pounded up the stairs. In the five weeks he'd been in Sweetwater, the atmosphere between his son and him had worsened. Dane hadn't thought that possible, but Blake resented him being one of the soccer coaches and went out of his way not to do what he asked at practice.

Zoey settled her bag of groceries on the counter. "Hi, Alex. Samuel. What brings you two by?"

"Dane had a great idea he wanted to talk to us about." Samuel stood, taking his mug to the sink. "He thinks we should start a youth center."

The widening of her eyes, the dropping of her jaw, accentuated her surprise. Dane's grip about his cup tightened. She might as well have advertised her feelings using a neon sign in the front yard. On his trip home to the United States all he could think about was starting over, wiping their past difficulties away. He should have known better. Like his recall of the plane crash—it just wasn't happening. Why couldn't it be that easy? Taking a mental eraser and cleaning off the slate in his mind? Because life wasn't easy. He knew that the hard way.

Alex, too, pushed to his feet and set his glass in the sink. "It's been needed for a while. It took someone new to Sweetwater to point that out."

An outsider. He'd always been one, even in Dallas, where he'd lived a good part of his adult life. His job hadn't been conducive to developing friendships because of the secrecy and travel involved in it. But during the past five weeks he'd gotten acquainted with Alex, and through him, Samuel. So when he'd come up with this brainstorm, they were the ones he'd immediately thought to tell.

Zoey withdrew the gallon of milk from the sack and put it in the refrigerator. "That's great," she finally responded.

Dane heard the tension in her words. The thin-lipped smile she gave Alex and Samuel reinforced Dane's notion something was wrong.

"We'd better get going." Samuel turned at the door into the kitchen. "Dane, I'll let you know what Wilbur and Nick say."

"Thanks. I'll talk to you two later. Alex, I'll see you at the game tomorrow." Dane started to walk them out.

Alex waved him still. "We've got it."

After the two men left, the tension in the room skyrocketed. The slamming of the cabinet drawer alerted him to a fight approaching. "Okay. Let's have it. What's wrong?"

Zoey crushed the bag into a ball. "How long have you been planning this youth center? Why do I hear about it from Samuel after you have shared it with them?"

Dane opened his mouth to say something but didn't know how to answer her.

She stalked to the trash can and stuffed the balled sack into it. "That's what's wrong. You don't share anything with me. I don't know what you're thinking." Spinning about on her heel, she planted a fist on her hip. "You can't even say anything now."

"I'm sorry. I didn't mean to exclude you. I

got this brainstorm this morning after you'd left for school."

Zoey gestured toward the front of the house. "But you called Alex at school, not me."

Hurt leaked through the anger in her expression, and Dane wasn't sure what to do. His husband skills were definitely rusty, maybe even nonexistent. He walked toward her, wanting her to understand he hadn't meant to leave her out of the loop. She backed up until the wall stopped her. Her arm fell loosely to her side, the rigid set of her body melting.

He started to clasp her upper arms and haul her against him. He wanted to hold her until— he just wanted to hold her. "I called Samuel this afternoon to get his take on the idea. He's the one who called Alex and they both came right over. It seems they had been kicking this same notion around for the past few months." He did finally brush his fingers down her arms then grasp her hands, tugging her to him. "I called. You weren't in your office."

"I didn't get any message you called." She tilted up her face, filled with confusion and that hurt he'd seen earlier.

"I didn't leave one. I knew you would be

home soon. In fact, I thought you would be here before Samuel and Alex arrived."

She dropped her head, staring at his chest. "I had to take Blake to get some supplies for a school project, then decided to do some grocery shopping while I was there."

He released her hands and wound his arms around her. "Well, what do you think?"

Again she looked him in the eye. "It's needed. Kids should have a safe place to go. A place where they can hang with their friends. There should be a counseling service available that they can tap into. Most of their problems go beyond school."

He caressed the length of her back. "Yeah, I know. I've dealt with the kids who turn to drugs to solve their problems. Rarely does it end well."

"They need other means available to help them." Zoey snuggled against Dane, relishing the moment of closeness with her husband. His interest and enthusiasm for the youth center was contagious. She hadn't seen him like this in a long time.

"Exactly. Want to volunteer at the center when it gets started?"

"I don't think it would be a good idea for me to do that at the center since some of those kids see me at school. I want them not to be afraid to talk to whoever is the counselor. They might not be able to see beyond me being the school counselor. Before you got involved in the DEA, that was your field. Have you considered doing something like that?"

A shadow crept into his expression. "No! I can't do that!" Dane stepped back, horror on his face.

His warmth gone, Zoey mourned its loss, at the same time grappling with the intense emotions flowing from her husband. "Why not?" *Tell me. Don't shut me out.*

"I'm more effective in law enforcement."

"Locking those kids up, not helping them stay off drugs?"

He plunged his fingers through his hair and turned away. "Yes, if you must know. I don't want to be responsible for someone else's problems. I'm not good at that. I can't even deal with my own."

Dane headed for the door. Zoey started to go after him, demand he tell her more. Something else was going on. She felt it in her gut. As usual her husband was holding back from her, not telling her the whole story. In college he had enjoyed his classes dealing with counseling and psychology.

Five minutes later, she heard the front door slam closed. She went into the living room and saw Dane, dressed in his workout clothes, quickly walking away from the house. In a little over a month's time he had built up his stamina until now he was jogging part of the way. His health was improving, but she didn't see any change in their relationship. They were two strangers sharing a house and children.

She leaned her forehead against the cool pane, closing her eyes. *Lord, help me. What do I do to get through to him? How can I help him when I don't know what is really wrong?*

Dane drove himself hard, his breathing coming in pants as his feet punished the pavement. He headed for the path by the lake even though it would be dark in half an hour. He couldn't tell her. He couldn't tell his own wife and see the pity and disappointment in her eyes. The one person he should have been able to help and he had failed his little brother. Some counselor he was. He couldn't even tell Jacob was in trouble and drowning. He couldn't tell he was on drugs and crying for help.

No, he was too involved with his classes and the counseling at the college clinic. Jacob's death from a drug overdose changed the direction of his life. He wasn't going to go back to being a counselor. He'd quickly figured that out when he had tried to help out at the halfway house. He was a law officer, determined to rid the world of as many drug dealers as he humanly could.

His lungs burned as he continued down the path alongside the lakeshore. But he wouldn't allow the pain in his chest to stop him. Maybe if he was exhausted in body and mind he could forget finding his brother's lifeless body in *his* bed as though Jacob had wanted to make a statement by overdosing in Dane's bedroom.

Jacob's image the last time he had seen him on the very bed Dane had slept in only two hours before flashed across the screen of his mind. Dane stumbled, caught himself before going down to his knees. He finally slowed his punishing pace to a jog, then a walk.

Coming to a halt, Dane leaned against an oak, gasping for air, his chest now ready to explode with his thudding heart. It didn't erase the memories—or the fact that he had let his little brother die. He should have seen the signs. He should have known Jacob was a drug addict.

No more! Dane shook his head, trying to rid

his mind of thoughts of the past. But still he remembered. He remembered holding his little brother in his arms, rocking him back and forth and willing him to wake up, tears he had never shed before or after running down his face. He had begged God not to take his little brother. But Jacob just lay limp, Dane's prayers gone unanswered. That was when he had vowed he would make the person who was responsible for selling Jacob the drugs pay. And he had, along with a whole score of others over the years as a DEA agent.

The beating of his heart decelerated and his breathing returned to an almost normal rate. Dane scanned the area where he was, the lake on one side of the path and a line of trees on the other, and realized he had never been this far before. Darkness closed in on him as he retraced his steps along the lake trail.

The sound of the water lapping the shore drifted to him. The scent of moisture and vegetation spiced the air. For a few seconds he was whisked back to the rain forest.

He saw houses lit in the distance and made his way toward them. Civilization. He was back in the States and he didn't feel like he fit in. He felt as out of place in Sweetwater as in the jungle.

He eased up on his pace even more when he hit the first residential street. He wasn't ready to go ho—to go back to Zoey's. He just couldn't call it home. He wanted it to be, but he was a stranger living in that house. Zoey felt that; he felt that.

Halfway down a long, dark road with an occasional house on either side, he heard tires screeching around the corner. Stepping off the pavement, he turned as a red Dodge Ram came barreling down the street, speeding past him. He only caught a glimpse of three of the plate numbers—five, three and eight—before the night obstructed his view.

At the end of the road the truck slowed to under the speed limit. Someone opened one of its back doors and the next thing Dane saw was a person flying out of the vehicle, landing on the side of the street and rolling down into the drainage ditch.

Dane barely noticed the truck as it accelerated again and flew around the corner. His arms and legs pumping, he raced toward the ditch, hoping the person was still alive. Adrenaline flowed through him, pushing away the exhaustion and renewed pain as he neared the scene.

A street lamp a few yards away cast a faint

light around the area, illuminating the ditch as he came up to it. Peering down, he prepared himself to jump into it when he heard a moan.

*He's alive.* Relief trembled through Dane. The person, face down in an inch of water, struggled to his knees and hands.

He slid down the embankment to help the teenager. Gripping one arm, Dane pulled him up as the boy jerked away, staggering back.

"Get away from me!" Eddy O'Neal shouted, his hands clenched.

In the dim light the only thing Dane could see was Eddy's face, a cut over his right eye bleeding, the other swollen nearly shut.

"Are you hurt?" Dane asked in a calm, authoritative voice, knowing full well he was but hoping his tone would placate the boy.

The teenager's raspy panting echoed through the silence. Worried, Dane took a step toward him.

"I said get away!" He backed up and nearly fell.

Dane held up his hands in front of him, palms outward. "Fine. I'll stay right here. Are you hurt?"

"No, I'm just fine. I tripped. That's all."

"I saw what happened. You didn't trip."

"I tripped!" the teenager yelled.

"Who was in the truck, Eddy?"

"Who are you?" The boy moved closer as if to get a better look at Dane in the faint light from the street lamp.

"I'm Dane Witherspoon."

"The narc?"

Dane stiffened at the sneer behind the teen's question. "Yes. Who was in the truck? Why were you thrown from it?" Keeping his voice steady, he watched the young man glance from side to side, then scramble up the incline and dart across the road.

With a sigh, Dane went after him, every muscle in his body protesting the further physical abuse. Eddy half limped, half ran toward a large house set back from the road. Dane caught up with him and managed to get in front.

"Eddy, you're hurt."

"You think! Gee, you are observant. I guess that comes from being a narc."

The teenager made the word *narc* sound dirty, as though he were spitting out a foul-tasting piece of food. "Where do you live?"

Eddy tried to move around him, stepped awkwardly on his right foot and crumbled to the ground. He cried out, pounding his fist into the dirt. "Get away! I can take care of myself."

Dane knelt next to him. "Where do you live?"

he asked in the firm voice that he had used a lot in the past—too many times.

The young man lifted his head, his face in the shadows. "Right behind you."

"Then I'll see you safely inside."

"No!"

"Yes. I'm not going anywhere until I make sure everything's all right."

"Do I look all right to you?"

"No, and that's the problem."

"Oh, man. My friends had to go somewhere and were late. I stumbled getting out of the truck. That was all there was to it." Slowly, with a stifled groan, Eddy pushed to his feet.

"I'm still seeing you home. I'm not going away."

Dane could feel, not see, the glare piercing into him as though the kid's eyes were two lasers cutting through a barrier—him. He waited patiently for Eddy to make the next move. Thankfully the teenager began to limp toward the house that had one light on in the front room. The porch was dark, and Eddy fumbled with his key for a good minute before he unlocked the door.

"Your father isn't home?" Dane asked, remembering Samuel telling him that day at church that Eddy's mother had left them.

"No," the teenager bit out through gritted teeth as he shuffled into his house, spinning around to close the door on Dane.

He stuck his foot in the entrance to stop it from shutting. "Where is your father?" He pushed his way into the house, the scent of stale beer accosting him. With a glance into the living room, he found the source of the smell. Empty cans littered the coffee table. "Did you and your friends have a little party earlier?"

Eddy drew himself up tall, his hands fisted at his sides. "If you don't leave, I'm calling the police."

Dane lifted his shoulders in a shrug. "Please do. They might be interested in what went on tonight. Drinking and driving."

"We weren't drinking and driving." Eddy pointed to a straight line made by the slats of the wooden flooring. "See, I can walk this line and not—" He fell to the side when he put his full weight down on his right leg.

Dane caught him. The teen wrenched himself free. If looks could kill, Dane noted he would be dead right now.

"Let me see your leg. Come on. You aren't getting rid of me."

Eddy gave him one more good glare before

hobbling into the living room and plopping down on the navy blue couch. He gingerly slid his pants up to reveal a long, nasty gash down his calf. Blood ran down his leg, pooling in his tennis shoe.

"You need stitches. How can I get ahold of your father?"

"My dad's at work."

"Where's your dad work?"

The teen's eyes widened. "You can't bother him."

Dane leaned closer, taking a whiff of Eddy's breath as he panted. No smell of alcohol. Inwardly Dane sighed with relief. The boy was in some kind of trouble, but at least he wasn't on drugs that he could tell or drinking alcohol—tonight.

"Why can't I bother him? He's your dad." Dane drilled his gaze into the kid's.

Eddy averted his head.

"Why, Eddy? What's going on here?"

"I—I—"

"Ed-dy—that you-uu?" a loud, masculine voice shouted from the back, his words slurred.

"Leave. Now before—" Eddy jerked to his feet, the look in his eyes pleading.

Dane slowly rose, his gut twisted into a huge

knot. "I'm staying. You need help." As he muttered his intent, Dane realized he would get to the bottom of what was going on with Eddy one way or another. This teen was screaming for help even if he didn't know it.

"Ed-dy!" The slurred voice came closer. "Have youuuu—"

A tall, thin man with several days growth of beard, his clothes rumpled and his eyes bloodshot, staggered into the entrance of the living room. He leaned into the door frame, clutching the wood for support. "Whooo's th-is?"

The man reeked of alcohol as if he had bathed in it. The smell turned Dane's stomach. Before he could move toward Eddy's dad, the teen hurried forward, propping his father against him.

"Dad, let me take you back to bed."

"Whooo…" The man's head slumped against his son's shoulder.

Eddy struggled to half drag, half walk his father down the hallway. Dane moved to the other side of Eddy's father and hoisted him up. The man swung his head around to look at Dane.

"Whooo…"

This time the man passed out. Dane helped Eddy drag him the rest of the way to the bedroom, then settle him onto an unmade bed. Beer cans overflowed on the surface of the two bedside tables. The muted TV showing a popular crime show was the only illumination in the room. While Eddy pulled the covers up, Dane turned the television set off.

At the door Dane said, "We need to talk."

Eddy backed away from the bed, then pivoted and rushed from the room. He stormed into the living room as best he could with a limp, then whirled around, anger in every line of his face. "Now you know. My father's a drunk."

"Okay, we can deal with that. You still need your leg seen to."

"I don't want anyone to know about my father's...problem. He'll lose his job if they do. He hasn't gone to work for the past two days. He called in sick."

"What's he do?"

"He's vice president of the bank. He can't lose his job. It would kill him."

"I think he's doing a pretty good job of that himself. He needs help. You need help."

Eddy's whole body went rigid. "We don't need anyone's help. My father doesn't drink much. He just got carried away this time."

Dane walked toward the phone on the end

table and started to pick it up when Eddy placed his hand over his on the receiver.

"I'm not going to the hospital and you can't make me."

Dane looked into Eddy's frightened gaze, then down at the boy's hand covering his. "My wife has a cousin who's a doctor. What if he meets us at his office—no one else around? I'm not leaving until I know you're all right."

Eddy's hand remained on his, a stubborn set to the teen's mouth.

"I'm calling my wife to get the number of her cousin. Okay?"

Fear flickered in Eddy's eyes. "Don't tell Mrs. Witherspoon about my dad or what happened tonight. Please."

"I won't unless you say it's okay." Suddenly it was important to Dane to gain this kid's trust.

The scared teen released his grip and stepped back.

Dane quickly placed his call. "Zoey, it's Dane."

"Where have you been?"

"Running. I needed to clear my head. Listen, I need Steven's number."

"Why?"

"I need to ask your cousin for a favor."

"What?"

"Nothing that concerns the family."

Zoey heard the evasive tone in her husband's voice and wanted to shout her frustration. Instead, she gave him Steven's number. "When are you going to be home? Do you want me to hold dinner?"

"I don't know and don't hold dinner. See you in a while."

Dane hung up the phone before Zoey could say another word. She slammed her receiver in its cradle, picked it up and slammed it down again.

"Mommy, what's wrong?"

Zoey spun around to face both Blake and Mandy in the kitchen doorway, worry on both their faces. She pushed her anger to the side to reassure her children. "Nothing, guys."

"But——" Blake said, his brows knitted.

"*Everything* is okay." She moved toward them. "Have you washed up for dinner?"

Blake nodded while Mandy kept her hands behind her back.

"Let me see, young lady."

Reluctantly her daughter held them out for her inspection. Smudges of blue paint were smeared across the backs. "Did you go out and start painting the house without your daddy?"

Mandy stared at the floor and mumbled her reply so low Zoey couldn't hear her.

"Amanda! What did you do?"

She yanked up her head, tears welling in her eyes. "Nothin'."

"This doesn't look like nothing." Zoey flipped over her daughter's hands to see the other side coated with the bright blue, too.

"I just opened the can to see the color he'd bought today."

"I told her not to. She doesn't listen to me." Blake walked toward the table, set for dinner.

"Why don't cha help us?" Mandy asked, her hands on her waist. "It would be done if ya did!" She jutted her chin up, glaring at her older brother.

Blake returned her glare, not saying a word.

Zoey gestured toward the sink. "Wash up now."

While Mandy stood on her stool and cleaned up, Zoey removed the setting for Dane and then sat next to Tara, who was happily eating a banana with half of it smashed on the tray.

"Where's Daddy?" Mandy asked, taking her chair across from Zoey.

"He has some business to take care of." *Which I have no idea what,* she silently added, feeling left out yet again in her husband's life.

Blake snapped his head around to stab Zoey

with a look of fright that he quickly masked, but his voice quavered as he asked, "He's working again?"

"No, honey. He's just delayed and will eat later."

This was the first indication in over a month that Blake even cared about his father. Samuel had tried counseling Blake and hadn't been successful, which had really concerned Zoey because Samuel was so good. She made a note to talk with her son later when Mandy wasn't around. Maybe now he was ready to open up.

The opportunity didn't present itself to Zoey until an hour later after Mandy had taken a bath to finish scrubbing the rest of the dirt and paint off her. Her look into the can of paint had been more than just a peek. Zoey had found a third of it spilled on the garage floor. Her daughter was going to bed early after helping Zoey clean up the mess.

"But, Mommy, I didn't mean to tip it over," Mandy protested as Zoey tucked her in. "Can I have a story?"

"Not tonight, young lady."

"But, Mommy—"

"Good night." Zoey switched off the overhead light.

The night-light illuminated the room in shadows, revealing her daughter wide awake, clutching her doll. "Mrs. Giggles wants her house finished."

Zoey quietly closed her daughter's door to her protests. Two children in bed, one to go. She knocked on Blake's door, intending to have that discussion with him. When he didn't say anything, she opened it to find her son curled in his bed asleep. He was becoming quite good at avoiding.

Zoey blew a long breath out and shut his door. Making her way downstairs to finish cleaning up the kitchen, she wondered where her husband was and what he was doing. She felt as if she were reliving the past when he would leave on an assignment and she knew nothing about what was going on. Her vivid imagination conjured up bad situation after bad situation. By the time he arrived home, she had become a basket case but tried to keep it from him. Whenever she'd expressed her worry early in their marriage, he'd clammed up even more about what was going on, as though not telling her protected her from the danger of what was happening.

As she wiped down the counters, a sound at the back door brought her around to face her husband.

He looked tired as if he'd finished running a marathon. His shoulders sagged, his eyes dull.

She tossed the washcloth into the sink and snagged his gaze. "Where have you been? And this time, I don't want any evasions."

## Chapter Eight

The exhausted look Dane sent her didn't sway Zoey. "What's been going on?"

He inhaled a deep breath, then released it slowly. Making his way to the sink, he filled a glass with water and downed it in several large gulps. "I can't tell—"

"I've heard that stock answer too many times. I'm not accepting it. You aren't working for the DEA at this moment."

He swung around to face her. "I made a promise to someone I wouldn't tell what happened unless he wanted me to. I *can* say I was helping out a teen who had gotten himself into a bind. It's nothing that affects this family and nothing to do with my job." He sank back against the counter, his hands gripping its edge.

"Your life revolves around secrets."

"Zoey, as a counselor, surely you understand the need to build trust and the need for privacy."

"You're counseling this person?" She remembered their argument earlier that had led to Dane's run.

"Not exactly, but he does need help."

"Okay," she answered slowly, hanging the wet washcloth over the sink. There was a part of her that understood Dane's need to keep this secret, but there was a part that was angry yet again that there was another mystery between them. "Do you want something to eat?"

"I'll fix a sandwich." He opened the refrigerator and took out the ingredients for it.

"Well, then I guess I'll go to bed." She started for the door.

"Don't. It's only nine. Stay and talk to me."

She froze for a few seconds, stunned by the offer. Unhurriedly she turned and shrugged. "Sure."

After he made a ham sandwich and poured himself a glass of milk, he sat across from her at the kitchen table. "After this incident this evening, I'm more convinced than ever that Sweetwater needs a youth center."

Zoey opened her mouth to ask why, but

instead snapped it closed. The subject was taboo, as were so many with Dane.

"This kid's having problems and really doesn't have anyone to go to."

"If he's in high school, he can come see me."

"I think the school environment can be stifling for some. Hopefully the center will be a place those teens who feel that way can connect with a counselor who can help. It just gives a troubled teenager another option."

"I'm all for that. I hope Samuel can work out the finances. Knowing Nick, he'll jump at the chance to fund it."

"I agree, from what I've seen of Jesse's husband." He took a bite of his sandwich, then washed it down with a drink of milk. "Maybe you can put in a good word tomorrow about the center at your little get-together. Are you meeting at Alice's Café?"

"Nope. Here."

"Here!"

"Don't act so panicked. It's just five women."

"You all are a force to be reckoned with." Suddenly Dane sat up straighter, his gaze glued to the window that overlooked the driveway. "There's something going on outside."

Zoey twisted around in her chair and saw the

flashing lights. Quickly she stood and headed for the front, Dane right next to her.

She reached for the handle, but Dane was quicker, opening the door and stepping out onto the porch before her. Parked three houses down at Wilbur Thompson's were two patrol cars, their red lights sweeping the darkness.

"You think it's another robbery or something else?" Zoey asked, trying to keep her alarm tamped down. This was too close to her own home.

"There's only one way to find out." He descended the steps and strode across the yard toward Wilbur's.

She closed the front door and followed. She arrived at Dane's side in time to hear Zach say, "Dad's house was broken into while he was at my place. He came home a while ago and found the window smashed, the back door standing wide open."

"Is your father okay?" Zoey asked, gripping Dane's arm, the very thought of someone coming into her house uninvited sending fear through her.

"Did you two see anything?"

Dane covered her hand and said, "I came home about twenty minutes ago but from the other direction. The street was deserted."

"They knew Dad wasn't home even though he had several lights on. Have either of you seen anyone suspicious around?"

"You think whoever did this was casing his house?" Dane thought of the red Dodge Ram and Eddy. Even at the doctor's office, the teen had refused to discuss what had gone on this evening that led to him being pushed from a moving truck. Was there a tie-in with the rash of robberies?

"Maybe. No one has been home with these break-ins. That's either extremely lucky or they have to be casing the places." Zach pocketed a pad.

"Do you know anyone who drives a red Dodge Ram with a partial tag number of 385?" Dane asked, aware of Zoey shifting beside him, her grip tightening.

Zach swung his full attention to Dane. "James Norton's son drives one. I've caught him speeding a few times. I don't know the tag number, though. Why?"

"Earlier, several streets over, I saw them joyriding, going twenty, thirty miles over the speed limit."

"Mmm. I'll check it out. Warn Clark that he has been sighted speeding on a residential street *again,* but with the kind of connections his father has that will be all I can do."

Dane heard the frustration in the police chief's voice and knew what the man was experiencing. "Who's James Norton?" Dane asked, hating the fact he didn't know very much about Sweetwater and its citizens. He felt at a disadvantage, much like he had in the Amazon. If he was going to help Eddy—and he had decided to whether the teen wanted him to or not—then he needed to know the people involved.

"He's the president of the biggest bank in town and doesn't let us forget it. He thinks money can solve any problem." Zach removed his pad again and wrote the partial tag number down.

"Son, they took my coin collection." Wilbur shuffled toward them. The old man slowed when he spied Dane, his eyes narrowing as his mouth curved into a scowl. "What are you doing here? My son doesn't need your *expert* help."

"Dad, please calm down," Zach said, walking toward his father to steer him away from Dane and Zoey.

"Let's get home." Zoey squeezed Dane's arm. "I don't like what's happened in Sweetwater. You aren't even safe in your own home."

Dane glanced at his wife, seeing the fear in her eyes and wishing it wasn't there. "This gang will be caught. They're getting bolder, robbing the police chief's father. They'll make a mistake."

"You think it's kids, don't you?"

Dane took her hand within his and strode toward the bright lights of her house. "Yes. My gut is telling me that Clark Norton has something to do with this."

"Why? He comes from a wealthy family. He doesn't need the money."

"People steal for other reasons than needing money."

"I can't believe Nancy's son would do something like this. She's Mandy's Sunday school teacher. Clark was just in my office last week about a schedule problem for next year. He's an excellent student with prospects of going to an Ivy League college."

"The Nortons go to Sweetwater Community Church?"

"Yes."

"I think I'll go with you this Sunday. I want to meet them."

"Did the speeding Dodge Ram have something to do with the incident you can't talk about?"

"Yes. Someone needs help and I'm gonna

give it to him, starting with checking out this Clark Norton at church."

Zoey didn't care why Dane was going to church with the family tomorrow. The fact that he was elated her. A ray of hope peeked through all that had happened lately. She hummed a current popular song while laying out the snacks and drinks for the get-together with her friends.

Mandy slammed open the back door and rushed inside. "Got to go." She raced through the kitchen, leaving the door wide open.

Zoey walked to it to close it and stopped in the entrance, shocked at the scene before her. Blake held a brush in his hand and was painting one side of the playhouse, not the same one as his father, but he was helping with the family project finally.

Dane glanced up and caught her look. He smiled. Her stomach flip-flopped. His smile was devastating, and often in the past could charm her out of her anger.

Mandy shot past her, nearly knocking Zoey down in her haste to get back outside. "Ya can hang the curtains soon, Mommy."

Zoey clutched the edge of the door to steady herself. Mandy took up her position next to

Blake, painting the lower part of the house while he took care of the top. Zoey's heart swelled at the picture of the three of them. She'd have to find out how Dane got Blake to help them.

Tara's voice could be heard over the baby monitor. It was time to get her youngest up from her nap so she could play with Rebecca, Darcy's daughter.

Fifteen minutes later, with Tara in her arms, Zoey opened the front door to her friends who had supported her when she had needed it the most. Once inside Darcy set Rebecca next to Tara on the floor in the center of the living room and the two toddlers played side by side. After drinks were poured and plates filled with goodies, the five women sat in a circle.

"Let's pray." Zoey took Beth's hand on one side and Tanya's on the other, then bowed her head. "Dear Heavenly Father, watch over these friends and their families. Help us and guide us through our everyday decisions and problems that arise. Through You we draw the strength we need. Through You we receive the love and forgiveness we ask for. In Jesus Christ's name. Amen."

"I heard the exciting news about the youth

center," Jesse said. "Nick has already decided to fund the start of the program."

Darcy and Tanya looked at each other with Tanya asking, "A youth center? This is the first I've heard of it."

"Samuel, Alex and Dane met yesterday about the center. Dane proposed it to them. Samuel has also called Wilbur about the building next door to the church. It looks like he'll give it to the program." Beth bit into a chocolate chip cookie.

"Wilbur!" Zoey and Darcy exclaimed together. "For free?"

"I know. I was surprised when Samuel told me right before I came over here. I think the robbery last night threw him off-kilter."

"The building needs a lot of work. I doubt he would have been able to do much with it." Darcy picked up a toy that Rebecca had tossed across the living room. "At least this way it won't completely fall into disrepair."

"Did you see Wilbur at the soccer game this morning? He didn't say two words. Most unusual. To think, he only lives a few houses down and he was robbed last night. I was here when it probably happened and didn't notice or hear a thing." Zoey shivered, remembering the two police cars out in front of Wilbur's, their red lights flashing as though warning the whole neighborhood of danger lurking.

"Yeah, I can remember when we grew up here in Sweetwater and our parents didn't bother to lock their doors." Jesse sipped her lemonade.

Tanya shook her head. "Not anymore. I double-check my doors before I leave the house."

"Well, for whatever reason we got the building and the funding, I'm glad we're going to have a youth center." Zoey thought of all the teenagers she counseled at school who could use a place to go. "Beth, did Samuel give you a timeline on the center?"

"I think he's looking at getting it up and running by the start of school next year, if not sooner. We'll have to find someone to run the center. Get the place fixed up and recruit volunteers."

"That's a tall order in four months," Jesse said. "Who could we get to do it? Samuel would be great."

"Samuel will help with it, but it would be too much for him to run the center and the church."

"Beth's right. The church is a full-time job." Darcy retrieved another toy that had flown across the room.

"How about Dane? It was his suggestion.

Didn't he study to be a counselor in college? That way he wouldn't have to go back to the DEA."

Darcy, Tanya and Beth nodded their agreement to Jesse's suggestion, all four of them peering at Zoey.

"I don't see him giving up his job with the DEA. That was his life before his disappearance," Zoey said, dreading the time her husband would go back to his old job. She couldn't see how it was going to work well with the family living in Sweetwater, even if Dane were assigned to the office in Louisville or Lexington.

"Maybe things are different and—"

The sound of the doorbell interrupted Beth. Zoey rose and went to answer it. Samuel stood on her front porch with a sad look on his face.

"Is Tanya here?" he asked.

Zoey knew something awful had happened by the solemn tone of his voice. "Yes. Is something wrong with Crystal?"

"No, it's her ex-husband. Tom died in a prison fight."

Zoey closed her eyes for a few seconds and sent a quick prayer to God for help for Tanya and Crystal. They had already gone through so much. Even though Tom had divorced

Tanya because he was in prison, she hadn't wanted him to but could do nothing to stop him from doing it, especially when Tom refused to see her.

"I'll go get her, Samuel." Zoey slowly walked into the living room, remembering her own time when she had been told by Dane's boss that he had disappeared. Then later Carl had come back to inform her that the government thought Dane had died. Each visit had sent a maelstrom of emotions raging through her.

"Who was that? I thought I heard Samuel," Beth said, looking toward the entrance.

"You did." Beth started to rise, and Zoey waved her down. "He needs to see Tanya."

All the color drained from Tanya's face. She opened her mouth, but no words would come out. Instead she forced herself to her feet and trudged toward the entryway.

Jesse arched her brow in question. Zoey mouthed the word *Tom* and hurriedly followed Tanya.

Samuel came to Tanya, took both her hands and said, "The prison called me about Tom. He was killed in a fight this morning."

Frozen, her eyes wide, Tanya stared through Samuel as if she hadn't heard what he'd said.

Zoey laid her hand on Tanya's shoulder and squeezed gently, wishing she could take her friend's pain away. No one could except the Lord. But she would be here for Tanya when she needed someone to talk to.

"I'll make the arrangements to have Tom's body shipped back here to be buried. You don't need to worry about that right now," Samuel said.

Finally Tanya blinked. "Thanks, Samuel. I— how am I going to tell Crystal?"

"I can come with you if you want," Zoey said before their minister could say anything. She remembered having to tell Blake and knew what Tanya was going through. Even though Crystal was older than Blake, the task would be difficult and heart-wrenching because Crystal loved her father.

Samuel caught Zoey's gaze. "Go with Zoey. I'll start working on the funeral arrangements."

"Okay," Tanya responded but didn't move.

"I'll go get your purse and drive you home. Dane can come pick me up later."

Now that Jesse was at Tanya's to sit with her, Zoey needed to go home and especially make sure that Blake would be all right with the news of Tom's death. Even though her son hadn't known Tom, Blake didn't handle death well.

Zoey felt as though she had been pulled and pushed in so many different directions. Tanya and Crystal's sorrow cut deep into her. Their sobs had ripped open a wound healed over time. Although Dane was alive, the emotions she had experienced inundated her all over again.

When the doorbell at Tanya's rang, Zoey rushed to answer it. Dane stood in the entrance, stiff, his brow creased.

"Is there anything I can do?" her husband asked, opening the screen door.

Zoey shook her head, going into Dane's embrace for a few seconds before stepping back. "We're all taking turns staying with Tanya. We don't want her and Crystal to be alone. As expected, they are taking it very hard."

Dane glanced beyond Zoey into the living room. Tanya sat on the couch, a vacant expression on her face, her eyes swollen from crying. Crystal, with her shoulders hunched, stared at her hands that she twisted over and over in her lap. "You went through this," he whispered, pivoting away from the scene of sorrow. "I'm sorry, Zoey, that you had to."

She quietly closed the front door and stopped

Dane from descending the steps. "You didn't do it on purpose."

He speared her with a mirthless look. "Do you *really* believe that?"

"Sure. Why would you ask that?"

"Because there are times I feel you blame me for being gone even though you've said you don't."

She started to protest his words, then realized he was right. In her mind she knew he'd had no control over what had happened to him in the Amazon, but in her heart she had blamed—still blamed—him. "I have. I'm the one who is sorry. I was wrong."

"But sometimes it's hard to change how you feel even when you know it's not right."

Tears close to the surface clogged her throat. "I'm trying."

He moved closer and cradled her face. "And I'm not making it easier for you."

"I could say the same to you." She leaned into his touch, needing the comfort he offered. Being with Tanya had brought back such painful memories of when she'd dealt with Dane's "death."

Standing on Tanya's porch, Dane bent forward, brushing his mouth over Zoey's, once, twice. Suddenly he drew her into his tight embrace and deepened the kiss, reaching into her heart and melting some of her defenses.

The hour was late, with one lone lamp on in the den next to Dane's sleeper sofa. The silence of the house should be a balm, but Dane strained to hear any sound that indicated others were near. All that greeted his ears was the patter of rain against the windowpane. A gentle washing of the earth.

Lying open in his lap was the journal he'd been keeping since he had returned to civilization that the psychologist in Dallas had suggested he do. He couldn't seem to get past noting Tom's death on the page, and yet something hopeful had happened today.

Blake had helped with the playhouse finally because his sister had begged him. He realized his son hadn't assisted because *he'd* asked him to, but he would take anything he could get. He'd actually seen Blake crack a smile earlier this afternoon at Mandy's feeble attempt to paint. The poor grass next to the playhouse was blue now instead of green.

More importantly, Blake had said a few civil sentences to him while they had worked. Dane rested his head back on the cushion, staring at the ceiling. Okay, so they were all concerned about the soccer game they'd played today, but it was a start.

And then Zoey and he had shared a moment on Tanya's porch. For the first time he felt he was making progress with his wife. If only it could continue. If only he could share more than a moment with her. What was he afraid of? Losing her if he admitted his failures?

Shutting the journal, he placed it in the table's drawer next to the couch. He'd write extra tomorrow night. Exhausted, his muscles protesting the painting he'd done, he slid down under the covers and closed his eyes. Sleep whisked him away in minutes....

*Heat scorched his skin. Lifting his head a few inches off the ground, he saw that he was trapped. A part of the plane crushed his legs. The red of the flames and the green of the jungle surrounded him as though they would be his coffin. He tugged. Pain shot through his body. Sagging back, he stared up at the trees above. The pressure on his legs pinned him down, sweat pebbling on his face as he drew in smoke-saturated air.*

*"Help!" His voice barely sounded over the*

*noise of the fire. From deep inside he pushed forth another cry. "Help!"*

*Struggling, twisting from side to side, he fought the confines of the prison that held him snared. "Help."*

From the distance a faint voice penetrated his desperation. "Daddy! Daddy, wake up."

The pressure on his legs moved to his chest, pressing him down. Mandy?

"Daddy, c'mon."

Small hands shook him. A finger poked his cheek. His eyes bolted open. His daughter sat draped over his chest, her gaze wide with fear, only inches from his face.

Her bottom lip quivered. "Ya scared me." Tears spilled from her eyes and rolled down her face.

One tear splashed onto him. He blinked, trying to rid his mind of the last vestiges of sleep that clung to him like road tar to a new car. "Honey, don't cry. I'm okay."

"Ya were yellin' for help."

"Just a bad dream. Nothing for you to worry about."

She sniffled. "I get bad dreams sometimes. Mommy helps me when I do. She'll make ya feel better. Do ya want me to go get her?"

*No!* his mind screamed. He didn't want to

drag Zoey into the nightmares he couldn't seem to shake. It was bad enough what she'd heard that one night; now his daughter had experienced one, too. He had to figure out what he wasn't remembering, what was eating at him. He didn't want to scare his daughter again.

"Honey, I'm fine." Dane glanced toward the window. He'd forgotten to pull the drapes, and outside dawn crept across the sky. "You're up early."

Mandy hauled Mrs. Giggles around and plopped her on his chest. "I wanna play in the playhouse."

Dane shoved himself up onto his elbows and managed to smile at his daughter. "It should be all dry by now."

Clutching her doll, she jumped from the bed. "Great! C'mon."

Laughing, he threw off the tangle of covers and rose. Mandy had a way of pushing his fears to the background. "Can I get dressed and have some coffee first?"

Mandy danced about. "Hurry. Hurry!"

"Tell you what. Why don't you go out and see if the paint is completely dry?"

"Sure." She flew out of the den, her shoeless feet silent on the floor.

At a slower, more sedate pace Dane tossed on a T-shirt and sweatpants, then ambled into the kitchen to start the coffee. The back door crashed open, Pepper racing into the house ahead of his daughter.

"It's dry! C'mon." Mandy hopped from one foot to the other.

Quickly, he plugged in the coffeepot while his daughter tugged on his pants. "I'm coming."

When he stepped out onto the deck, he realized he was as barefooted as his daughter. The early morning chill sent a jolt of alertness through him. He turned to go back in for his tennis shoes, but Mandy kept pulling him toward the playhouse.

At the window Mandy peered inside. A frown knitted her brow. "Daddy, there's someone sleepin' in my house."

## Chapter Nine

"What!" Alarm zipped through Dane, thoughts of the recent break-ins alerting him to danger. Pulling Mandy away, he pressed close to the window, staring into the playhouse. Lying on the floor, his head cushioned by his arm, was Eddy O'Neal, his eyes closed in sleep. "What's he doing here?"

Mandy tugged on his T-shirt. "Who is he, Daddy?"

Twisting around, Dane placed a hand on his daughter's shoulder. "Mandy, will you go in and check to see if my coffee has finished perking? I'll be inside in a minute. You wait in the kitchen. We'll have some breakfast together."

"But, Daddy—"

He spun Mandy toward the back door and said, "Mandy, go inside while I talk with Eddy."

She turned toward Dane and tilted her head. "Is he in trouble?"

Good question. "I don't know, hon. Now go."

Reluctantly Mandy trudged toward the deck, glancing back several times. Dane stood by the entrance into the playhouse and waited until his daughter had disappeared inside. Heaving a sigh, he thrust open the door and entered. The teen remained asleep, curled on the floor, his white bandage over his eye in stark contrast to his unruly long, dark hair.

Dane squatted next to the boy and nudged him in the shoulder. Eddy flinched, his eyes snapping open. He scrambled away, his back hitting the wall. Bringing his legs up, he clasped them to his chest, his gaze riveted to Dane.

"What are you doing here?" Dane calmly asked, for a few seconds feeling as though he were talking to a child Blake's age rather than a sixteen-year-old.

Eddy's frown wiped the shocked look from his face. "I needed a place to stay. This looked as good as any."

"Yeah, and I believe that story about as much as your one about tripping as you got out of the truck the other night. Now are you going to be straight with me or are we going to dance around the issue until you finally tell me what's going on?"

Eddy shifted his gaze to the window, a question entering his eyes. "What time is it?"

"Almost six."

"I've got to get going." Eddy shot to his feet. Slowly Dane rose, blocking the teen's escape. "Not before you tell me why you decided to spend the night in my daughter's playhouse."

"Did anything happen last night?"

Dane narrowed his gaze on the boy. "Like what?"

He shrugged his slender shoulders. "Oh, I don't know."

"Sure you do or you wouldn't have asked. What's going on?" Dane pronounced each word of the question slowly.

"I—I overheard someone talking about making you pay for telling the police about them speeding." Eddy kept his gaze trained on the window to the left of Dane.

"Would this someone be Clark Norton?"

The teenager nodded.

"What was Clark planning?"

Another shrug.

"Eddy, is Clark behind these break-ins? Are you involved?"

"No!" The teen's attention swung around to Dane. "I don't steal. I don't know what Clark and his friends do. They were just angry that the police chief came to visit them today, I mean yesterday."

"Why were you here? Did you think you could stop them?"

Eddy's head dropped. "I was gonna try," he mumbled, his look boring a hole in the floor. "But it started raining and I got sleepy. Nothin' happened?" He lifted his gaze to Dane.

"No, at least I don't think so." Dane reached for the teen, clasping his shoulder. "C'mon in and have some breakfast with Mandy and me before you head home." Looking at the boy's slim body, Dane wondered how good the teenager's diet was. With no mother and a father who was drinking, he feared that Eddy had to look out for himself a lot of the time. He knew what that was like.

"I should—"

"Please."

"Okay." Eddy shuffled out of the playhouse and then followed Dane toward the house.

When Dane opened the back door, he found

Mandy standing on the stool at the stove helping Zoey prepare some pancakes. Zoey glanced at them. Mandy peered around her mother to get a look at the teenager.

"This is Eddy, Mandy."

His daughter grinned, hopped down from the stool and came over to them. "How'd ya like my playhouse? Daddy built it for me."

"Nice," Eddy mumbled, not looking at Zoey.

"I've invited Eddy to have breakfast with us." Dane walked to his wife, seeing the confusion in her eyes. "Can I help with anything?" He leaned close and kissed her on the cheek, whispering, "I'll explain later."

She masked her questions and said, "You set the table and pour the orange juice. The pancakes are almost done."

"Mommy makes the bestest pancakes, Eddy." Mandy took the teen's hand and led him to the sink. "We always hafta wash our hands before we eat. Ya go first."

Dazed, Eddy did as the five-year-old commanded. Dane suppressed his laugh at the way his daughter had taken over.

"He was the one you were with the other night?" Zoey asked when the kitchen was finally cleared of their children and Eddy, who had gone home.

Dane lifted his mug to his lips and took a long sip. When he put it on the table, he looked at her. "Yes."

"What's going on? He has a black eye and a bandage over the other, and I noticed he was limping. What happened the other night? Did he get into a fight?"

Dane studied the contents of his mug. "Honestly, I'm not sure what went on. I don't think there really was a fight. I think it was totally one-sided, with Eddy on the wrong side."

"Who did that to him?"

"I believe Clark Norton and a few of his buddies."

Zoey sucked in her breath. "Clark? He can be a bit reckless, but all the kids seem to like him. As I said earlier, he's an A student."

"I know what I saw. I saw Eddy being pushed from a moving truck—Clark's moving truck."

Shock rendered Zoey speechless. She couldn't rid her mind of the picture of Eddy tumbling from Clark's red truck. "Why?"

"I'm working on that. Eddy isn't too forthcoming." Dane started to say something, stopped and glanced away.

"Is there more?"

"It isn't my place to tell you. It's Eddy's story."

"You promised him you wouldn't say anything?"

Dane nodded, cradled his mug in his hands and sipped at his coffee.

"What's going on in Sweetwater, Dane?"

"Have the Nortons lived here long?"

"About a year. Clark's father was transferred to the bank and promoted to president. They've been active at the church and prominent in community activities."

"Well, I think they have a son who is trouble."

"Is he why you want to come to church?"

"Yep. I want to meet this Clark Norton. Size him up."

"You sound like you're going to war."

Dane rose and leaned forward, his fists resting on the table. "I'm gonna fight for Eddy."

"Fight?"

"I don't mean physically. Eddy needs a friend who'll stand up for him, help him."

"Eddy has a father."

Dane snorted and made his way toward the sink to put his mug in it.

"Dane, what's wrong with Eddy's father?" Zoey stood and faced her husband.

"Let's just say the man has his own problems."

"Yes, I know about his wife running out on him. That has to be tough." She'd had a taste of what it felt like to be abandoned, even though Dane hadn't chosen to leave them.

"He has a son who's hurting, too. He should…" Dane's voice faded into the silence. "Listen to me." He closed his eyes, lowering his head. "We could be talking about Blake."

"Yes."

Dane pivoted toward the counter, pressing into it as though it were the only thing holding him up. "I'm as guilty as Eddy's dad. I've torn this family apart and done nothing to put it back together." He scrubbed his hands down his face as though trying to wipe something from his mind.

The agony in Dane's voice conveyed the emotions swamping her. Trembling, she clasped his shoulder. "Let me in. Let me help you, Dane. What happened in the Amazon?"

"I don't remember. That's the problem. I know something bad happened and I can't remember it."

"Yes, something bad happened. Your plane went down."

He shook his head. "No, before that." He

turned toward her. "I just don't know what and it's eating at me."

She laid her palm over his heart, feeling it pound beneath her touch. "Don't try so hard. It doesn't make any difference now. You're home safe."

"A chunk of my life is gone. For a man who likes to be in control, I feel helpless."

She'd always known control was important to him. "Control is an illusion."

"I don't accept that we don't have choices in our life."

"I'm not saying that. I've seen too many times I thought I had things under control, and I never really did. But when you turn your life over to the Lord, you put control in His hands. Your choices are guided by Him."

He covered her hand on his chest. "I don't know how to turn my life over to anyone."

She wanted to make him see how easy it could be if only he would trust the Lord. Then control wouldn't be what was so important to him. "It isn't easy. You have to allow Christ into your heart. Put your faith totally in Him."

"I've seen so much evil in this world, Zoey."

The fact that Dane was discussing God with her, sharing his feelings some, spurred her to say, "All the more reason to believe in God. There's good all around us."

"And bad."

"You always did say the glass was half empty rather than half full. We'd better get ready for church. You're still coming, aren't you?" For a few seconds her breath caught in her lungs as she waited for his answer, hopeful he still was going with them.

"Yes, but first I want to have a few words with Blake. I've left him alone too long. I know that now."

"I'll get Mandy and Tara ready to go. We need to leave in forty-five minutes."

"I'll be ready."

"Do you think Eddy will be at church? He used to come a lot when his mother did. Now he only comes occasionally."

"I don't know, Zoey." Dane headed for the stairs and his necessary conversation with his son.

He knocked once on Blake's door, paused a few heartbeats, then entered his room. His son sat at his computer playing a game. He glanced toward him, frowned and continued to move his man through a maze.

"Can we talk?" Dane asked, sitting on the messy bed behind Blake.

His son battled a monster, lost and died.

Dane waited.

Blake swung around in his chair, hugging its back.

"First, I wanted to thank you for helping to paint the playhouse yesterday. We were able to finish it in time so it could dry before the rain started."

"I did it for Mandy."

"I know. But I still appreciated the help."

"Sure." Blake started to turn back to his computer.

"*Second,* I think we should talk about my disappearance and reappearance."

His son's grip on the back of the latticed chair tightened. He shifted his gaze back to Dane. "You were in the jungle. What's there to talk about?"

"How you felt. How you feel now. You're angry with me. You think I let you down, but son, I would have done anything to get back here if I had remembered you all."

Blake veiled his eyes. "How could you forget us?"

"I had suffered severe injuries, including a head injury, from the plane crash. I was lucky to even be alive, but I couldn't remember much for a long time. Slowly memories started coming back to me—more like flashes, but still I couldn't seem to put it all together until the *National Geographic* team came into the village. Then things started to fall into place. I didn't forget on purpose. I had amnesia. You know what amnesia is?"

Blake didn't say anything. He hunched his shoulders as though he were curling in on himself.

Dane's heartbeat slowed, a great pressure bearing down on his chest. "It's when you don't remember parts or all of your previous life. Traumas to the head can cause your brain to swell, to block part of your life from your memory. Sometimes your memories come back quickly, all at once. Sometimes slowly in bits and pieces. Sometimes not at all." He thought of the few remaining gaps in his memory and wondered if they would ever be filled in.

Blake sniffed, rubbing his hand across his nose. But Dane saw the tears leak out of his son's eyes. Dane knelt in front of Blake, compelling his son to look at him.

"I love you, Blake."

His son's tears continued to pour from him. "You don't hate me for telling you I didn't care if you ever returned?"

Dane recalled the fight they'd had that last

night before he'd gone to South America. He wasn't going to see his son perform the lead in his class's music program in two days. Blake had angrily shouted those words at him as he'd come to tell his son good-night and wish him good luck in the program. He would be gone before Blake got up the next morning. Dane had left knowing Blake was upset. He'd been determined to make it up to his son when he returned. He'd never gotten the chance—until now.

Dane leaned up and took Blake into his embrace. "I love you. I could never hate you. We all say things we don't mean from time to time, especially me."

With tears flowing down his cheeks, his son flung his arms around Dane's neck. "Dad, I thought I had made you go away, that you weren't coming back because of me."

His own tears choked Dane's throat, making it impossible to say anything for a moment. "You couldn't keep me away." He gave his son a squeeze then moved back. "Never."

Blake drew in deep breaths, blinking several times. "I didn't mean the words."

"I know." Dane wiped the last of the tears from his son's cheeks. "Now if we don't get dressed for church, your mother won't be too happy with us."

"You're really going to church with us?"

Dane shoved himself to his feet. "You bet. It's about time I got more involved in what's going on around here." As he declared that to his son, he realized he meant every word. He'd been licking his wounds too long—the past five weeks—and he did need to get a better handle on his life.

After the service in the rec hall at Sweetwater Community Church, Dane refilled his mug with coffee, then stepped away to allow Samuel to do the same. "I'm glad things are falling into place concerning the youth center."

"Faster than I imagined. It seems a lot of people had been thinking about doing something like that, but it took you to bring it out into the open." Samuel moved toward the far wall where it wasn't as crowded. "I'm going to take a look at the building on Tuesday. Want to come along?"

"Sure. I'm not doing anything else." And that was the problem. He needed to make some decisions about what he wanted to do. He was feeling much better, his strength almost totally returned. He needed to call Carl this week. He needed to talk to Zoey about it.

"Good. I'd like your opinion on what needs to be done."

"I would like to talk to you about my nightmares. Mandy got scared when she heard me this morning. I don't want to frighten my children, but I don't seem to have much control over when they occur." Dane didn't know what else to do. The memory of Mandy's fear earlier when he'd awakened from his nightmare impaled him with urgency. He would do anything not to have a repeat of that—even talk to someone about the dream.

"I'm always available if you'd like to talk. How about after we look at the building?"

"That would be great. Maybe then I could get a handle on these dilemmas plaguing me."

"We all have problems."

Dane saw Zoey threading her way through the crowd. She smiled and headed toward them. Seeing her caused his heart to beat faster. She was a beautiful woman inside and out. He was lucky to be married to her, and yet there was so much that was wrong with their marriage. How could he fix it? How could he recapture the closeness they'd had once?

"You two look like you're conspiring." Zoey stopped next to Dane.

"Making plans for the youth center. I'm going with Samuel to inspect the building on Tuesday."

"I'd better have a word with Mr. Norton before he leaves. See you on Tuesday, Dane." Samuel walked toward a tall, distinguished-looking man standing with several others, gesturing with his hands as he talked.

Dane studied the banker, remembering when Zoey had pointed out his son earlier to him. Clark looked a lot like his father, tall for his age with brown hair, cut conservatively, and pleasing features that probably charmed the girls. But beneath the easy smile the teen used too much, Dane had seen a hardness in his expression.

"Dane, are you okay?"

Zoey's words came to him, pulling him away from his thoughts. "Sorry, thinking about Clark. He's trouble, Zoey."

"I noticed Eddy didn't come to church."

"That I intend to change. I'm gonna invite him to come with us next week."

"You're coming next week?" Zoey's smile grew.

"Yep. This weekend I made a decision to become involved. No more hiding out at home."

"I noticed Blake was talking to you on the way to church."

"We actually had a good conversation this

morning. He thought I had stayed away because right before I had left for South America, he had told me he didn't care if I returned."

"He never said anything to me. So *that's* what has been eating at him."

"Yep. I reassured him that I loved him no matter what. I think it's a new beginning for us."

*What about us?* Zoey thought, mixed emotions twisting together to knot her stomach. She was happy Dane and Blake had mended their relationship, but sadness leaked through. Watching her husband scanning the rec hall for their son, she wished their problems could be solved with a simple clearing up of a misunderstanding. Life was rarely that easy. "I came over here to get you so we can leave. Mandy has been bugging me since church was over to go home. She wants to play in her new playhouse with Mrs. Giggles and Pepper. So are you ready to go?"

"Just say the word and we're out of here." Dane began to make his way toward his children with her next to him.

Mr. Norton stepped in his path. "Nick told me about the new youth center. I'd like to contribute to it."

Zoey saw the tensing of her husband's shoulders and the flattening of his mouth a few seconds before he smiled and shook the man's hand in greeting.

"Samuel and Nick are handling that. Any donation is appreciated," Dane replied in an even voice.

The tight thread that ran through her husband's words prompted Zoey to say, "Thanks, James. This center will be important to the town. Honey, we'd better get going." Then to the banker, she added, "We have a very full afternoon." Taking Dane's elbow, she steered him toward Blake and his group of friends.

"Dad, Craig was telling us about the youth center we're gonna have."

Dane clapped his hand on his son's shoulder. "Yep, hopefully by the end of the summer. We're gonna renovate the building next door to the church."

"Can we help? Dad said he thought there would be some jobs we could do," Craig said, nodding to his friends. "What do you all think?"

A couple of the boys murmured their agreement, which sparked Dane to say, "I think that's a great idea. Since you'll benefit the most, it seems appropriate you have a say in how the center is renovated."

"Are you gonna head it up?" Blake asked, an eagerness in his expression.

"I—I don't think so. It'll be a full-time job for someone."

Blake frowned. "But you're not working right now."

"I will be soon. I have to go back to my job. My leave is almost over."

Listening to Dane's announcement, Zoey stiffened. She'd known he would be returning to work but had hoped it wouldn't be this soon. "When?"

Dane glanced at her, a shadow creeping into his eyes. "I need to call Carl this week. Set up a time to go to Dallas and discuss my future."

When her husband returned to the DEA, everything would go back to the way it was before he'd left for South America. When Dane did a job, he put his all into it. That was one of the things she loved about him, his passion and dedication, until it had almost destroyed their marriage. "I see. Well, let me know when you decide to leave." Her tone chilly, she turned away to find Mandy.

Zoey located Mandy with Allie and Cindy. She left her son and husband to round up her middle child and get Tara from the nursery. Disappointment shook her body. When Dane had talked about becoming involved, she'd allowed herself to dream that he would stay in Sweetwater and find a job here, not one with the DEA. She should have known better. His whole life was his work and that wasn't going to change even if other aspects of him did.

"We can gut this first floor to put in a gym, taking some of the second story over there." Samuel pointed to the back of the building. "I have a member of the church who volunteered to go through the building and make sure it's constructively sound before we get started."

"Good. I would hate to start tearing out walls and have the place fall down around us." Dane walked toward the set of double front doors.

"I'm getting a lot of people coming forward to volunteer their expertise, which will cut the cost some."

"We can put what we save into the equipment and furniture for the center."

"You keep saying 'we.' Have you reconsidered heading up the center?"

Dane stepped outside, the bright spring sunlight making him squint after being inside the darkened building. "I'll do what I can when I'm not working, but I talked to my boss in Dallas this morning. I'm flying down there next week."

"To start work?"

He took a deep breath, the air laced with the scent of mowed grass and flowers. "We're going to discuss my options. He's going to bring me up to speed concerning the drug operation I was investigating that sent me to South America. I spent three years working on that case. He didn't tell me much when I first came back from the jungle." Dane followed Samuel, who crossed the yard to the church. "I feel like I have unfinished business involved with my job."

"So you don't have a choice in going back?"

"Yeah."

"How does Zoey feel about this?"

"She's not too happy. I haven't told her yet that I talked with Carl this morning. I thought I would when she got home tonight. It's not something I want to tell her over the phone." He'd wished he could put it off until right before he had to leave. The thought of telling Zoey made him hope he could find the right words. But he didn't know if that was possible, since every time he contemplated the future, confusion gripped him.

In the Garden of Serenity, Samuel paused and

indicated a bench. "I can't pass up such a gorgeous day. When spring comes, I love to be outside as much as I can."

Dane took a seat across from Samuel, the sound of a bird chirping above him drawing his attention for a moment while he tried to gather his thoughts. He wasn't used to talking to someone about his feelings. Where did he begin?

"You said something about Mandy being scared because of your nightmare. Why don't you tell me about this dream?"

Relieved that Samuel had taken the lead in this counseling session, Dane directed his gaze at the minister and said, "It's always the same. The plane crashes and I'm trapped in a fire. I'm pinned down and can't get out. I always wake up, though, before the flames consume me completely, usually in a cold sweat, the covers twisted around me as if I'd fought them, and I'm often calling out."

"That's what Mandy saw?"

"'Fraid so."

"Why do you think you keep dreaming this?"

"I'm not sure. I guess because I don't know what happened in the plane before we crashed."

"And you think something important happened?"

Dane nodded, seeing in his mind's eye a blurry outline of someone, as though he were looking at a person through a windshield in the pouring rain and the wipers weren't working. "I keep seeing a gun pointed at me, but I can't tell who was pointing it or even if it really happened."

"How many were on the plane?"

"Myself, the pilot and my partner."

"So do you think the pilot or your partner pointed a gun at you?"

Dane looked away, watching the leaves on a maple tree fluttering in the gentle breeze. "I would have said no. Bob and I had worked together for several years. I thought I could trust him, but why do I keep seeing the gun? Was someone else there with us, holding us hostage? Why did the plane go down?"

"You need to ask yourself why it's so important for you to know that now. Will it change anything? The pilot and your partner are dead. Even if one of them caused the crash, there's nothing that can be done about it. Do you want it to govern the present? Your future?"

"Why did I survive the crash? I shouldn't have! I should have died with them." Dane couldn't shake the feeling he should have died with the other two. His survival plagued him. Maybe that was the cause of his nightmare—guilt.

"God had other plans for you."

"But I don't know if I have it in me to continue my fight against drugs." Dane finally admitted what had been bothering him since returning to the United States. His battle against drug dealers had been his life's work. What would he do without it? He felt lost and adrift, going through each day without a purpose.

"Maybe He doesn't want you to. Ridding the world of drugs is a noble cause, but there are others, too. Have you talked with Zoey about any of this?"

Dane rested his elbows on his thighs, clasping his hands between his legs. "No. I don't know what to say to her. I don't want to let her down, but..." He couldn't finish his sentence, fear of being unable to do what his wife needed clutching him. He was used to action, not words.

"What you said to me is a good start. Share this with her. Get her input on it."

*Share.* Dane nearly laughed at that word. "According to Zoey, I don't know how to share. At least not my feelings."

"What do you think?"

"She's right. How do you start when you never have?"

"One feeling at a time. Start with something you are comfortable sharing. You don't have to do it all at once."

Dane did laugh this time. "If I did, Zoey would go into shock."

"You said you had to tell her about the trip to Dallas. Start with that and how you feel about going."

Sliding his hand back and forth across his nape, Dane shook his head. "That's a tough one. I don't know how I really feel."

"Then explain what you can. Women are more comfortable expressing their emotions than men, usually." Samuel grinned. "But they expect us to."

"Yeah, I know." After rolling his shoulders to work the tautness out, Dane pushed to his feet. "I'd better get home. Blake will be home from school soon, and I promised him I would work with him on passing the soccer ball around."

"Glad to see things are better there."

"Me, too. It was getting mighty cold at my house."

Dane strolled the few blocks home, enjoying the beauty of a crystal clear blue sky and a perfect temperature in the midseventies. So different from the jungle, where he would have been dripping wet after a walk of the same distance. Just as he was getting used to the Amazon, he'd found himself back in the States, having to acclimate to a whole new town and house—and for that matter, a new family with the addition of Tara.

He grinned, thinking of his youngest as he mounted the steps to his front porch and unlocked his door. Both of his daughters were at their grandmother's while he met with Samuel. Their treat this evening was to have dinner with Nana.

The phone ringing cut into his thoughts. He hurried to answer it in the kitchen.

"Dad, Craig and I have a science project due this week at school. Is it okay if I stay at his house and work? Mrs. Morgan asked me to dinner. Can I?"

"Sure. I'll come by and pick you up, say, at eight."

"'Kay."

So he and Zoey would be alone for a few hours tonight. A rarity in a house with three young children, but one he would use to his advantage. He laid out some steaks to thaw in cold water while he checked the refrigerator for the makings of a salad and baked potatoes. He could cook dinner and surprise Zoey.

He made a tossed green salad and was washing off the potatoes when Zoey came into the kitchen through the back door. She looked tired. He finished what he was doing and turned toward her as she flipped through the stack of mail on the desk.

"How was your day?"

"Long. I went by to see Tanya and Crystal on the way home. She's holding up pretty good, but Tanya is concerned about Crystal being at the funeral tomorrow."

"Why?"

"She won't talk about her dad, not even with Tanya."

"Like Blake?"

Zoey nodded. "It isn't good to keep your feelings inside. They have to come out somehow."

*And I keep mine inside,* Dane thought, having always had a hard time expressing himself to anyone, even Zoey. Was that what he'd done wrong with his little brother? Not let him know how much he loved him?

"Eddy came to see me." Zoey put the stack of mail back on the desk next to her purse.

"He did?"

"He wanted to thank me for breakfast the other day. When he lingered, making small talk, I knew he wanted something else."

"What?"

"To talk about his mother."

"Not his dad?"

"I know his father is drinking too much. He told me."

"Good. I didn't like not telling you, but it needed to come from Eddy. Is there anything you can do for him?"

"I'm hooking him up with our drug and alcohol counselor to get the support he needs to deal with his dad's alcoholism." Zoey peered around Dane. "What have you been doing?"

"Fixing dinner."

Both of her brows rose in surprise.

"Okay, it isn't much, but it's a start. I've got a salad. I'll put the potatoes in the microwave like I've seen you do, and I'll grill two steaks for us."

"Two? What about Blake?"

"Eating at Craig's. That leaves us alone this evening."

"Oh."

"A novelty, isn't it? We could consider this our second date."

"At least people won't be staring at us." She headed for the hallway. "I'm gonna change. Be back in a few minutes, and I'll set the table."

While Zoey was gone, Dane seasoned the steaks and prepared them for the grill. He stuck the potatoes in the microwave, ready to bake when he put the meat on to cook. But first, he wanted to tell Zoey about going to Dallas. He didn't want it hanging over his head the whole way through dinner.

"What time do we need to get Blake?" Zoey asked when she came back into the kitchen.

"I thought I could pick him up at the same time I pick the girls up, at eight."

"Two hours. It's hard to get two hours to myself."

"You don't have two hours to yourself. I'm here." It would be so easy not to say anything to her, to savor this time alone, he thought but realized he couldn't keep putting off the inevitable. With determination Dane crossed the room to her and clasped her hands. "Come. Sit down. I want to talk to you before we eat."

Warily, Zoey allowed him to tug her toward the kitchen table. He pulled out the chair for her. After she sat, he took a seat next to her, his gaze connecting with hers.

"I talked to Carl this morning."

A frown lined her full lips, but she didn't say anything.

"He wants me in Dallas by the middle of next week."

She blanched and shoved the chair back, standing. Her hands fisted on the table, tension in every line of her body. "So soon? You haven't even been here six weeks."

"It must be your great cooking. I'm feeling so much better and I've gained quite a bit of my weight back."

"Gee, I'm glad I could help you get better so you could leave again." Zoey whirled around and fled the kitchen.

## Chapter Ten

Dane caught Zoey halfway to the back door.

A suffocating pressure squeezed her chest. She shook his hand off her. She needed fresh air. She escaped outside onto the deck as the sun began its descent toward the line of trees along the back of her property. Forcing rich oxygen into her lungs, she leaned against the railing, trying to get a handle on her swirling emotions.

*He's leaving.*

*Again.*

*Why? When I finally thought we might have a chance?*

*Lord, I don't understand. Help me. I can't go back to Dallas. I can't live that life again.*

She dropped her head, staring at her hands gripping the wooden railing so hard her knuckles were white. He'd started going to church, talking with Samuel. Dane's relationship with Blake had improved and he had shared a few things with her. That had been progress. All gone because once his job consumed his life the family would come in second.

The back door opened. "Zoey. Talk to me."

She laughed and heard the almost hysterical ring. "I can't believe you have the nerve to say, 'talk to me.' This from a man who doesn't understand the concept of a two-way conversation about anything having to do with feelings."

Dane covered the area between them in three strides, moving into her personal space until she had to back up, trapped in the corner of the deck.

"I have unfinished business I have to take care of. I don't know what I'm going do about my job. If I continue with the DEA, it would be here in one of the offices in Kentucky. I won't ask you to move to Dallas. Sweetwater is good for our family."

"Why do you have to work for the DEA?"

His chest expanded with a deep breath he blew out in a rush. "I have to do what I can to stop drugs from taking over. I—"

"There are other ways than throwing yourself one hundred percent into your job, putting your life constantly on the line. Isn't two-and-a-half lost years enough?"

"You knew my dedication to my work when you married me."

*Yes, but not the all-consuming part,* she thought. *Not the part where you become lost somewhere deep inside because of what you deal with day in and day out. Not to the point myself and the children come in second.* "The job changed you over the years."

"I'm still the same guy you married."

"Are you? I saw a man who spent more and more time on the job. I saw a man miss one family function after another. I saw a man who wasn't around for two of the births of his children because of his work. I saw a man turn inward until he didn't share anything with me. You came home and didn't want to talk about your work, nothing."

He jerked back, combing his hand through his hair. "Because it was always so ugly. Not something I wanted to share with you and the kids. I didn't want to bring it into my home. I wanted to forget it for a little while. I didn't want to drag you into that world."

"If that was where you were, then that was where I wanted to be."

"But I don't want you there."

"We are supposed to be partners, but I don't feel that way. Remember the vows we took? 'For better or *worse.*'"

"What's wrong with me wanting to protect you and the kids from the ugly side of life?"

"It doesn't work if in the process we lose you."

He turned away, striding toward the door. "I haven't committed to anything yet. I'm going to talk with Carl. That's all. I'd better get the steaks on if we're gonna eat before we have to pick up the kids."

The door banged closed. Zoey stared at it, thinking that it was symbolic of their relationship. He had shut the door yet again on her getting too close. A silent scream welled up in her that she was so tempted to release. She didn't. She trapped it inside as she did so much of her frustration.

As he brought the steaks out, she made her way into the house to set the table. She needed to keep busy, focus her thoughts on something other than Dane's trip to Dallas next week. *Lord, I'm turning this problem over to You. Please guide me in what I need to do to make this marriage work.*

"Where are the kids?" Zoey asked when she came into Tanya's kitchen.

Jesse motioned in the direction of the backyard. "Outside. Hopefully distracting Crystal."

"Tanya said she hasn't eaten a thing today."

"Well, then I'll fix a sandwich for her. There's certainly enough food here."

Zoey scanned the counters that were laden with casseroles, the makings of different kinds of sandwiches, salads, desserts and large pitchers of iced tea and lemonade. "Tanya won't have to cook for a month at least with what the people from the bank and church have brought by."

"I think she was surprised at some of the people who came by."

Zoey moved closer and leaned toward Jesse to whisper, "Yeah, James Norton, the president of the bank, is in there right now talking with Tanya. He couldn't come to the funeral earlier, but he wanted to pay his respects."

"Well, I'll be. Never thought he had time for us. I get the feeling he doesn't like living in Sweetwater."

"I get that impression with the whole family."

Jesse picked up the plate with a turkey sandwich and chips. "I'll check on the kids and sit with Crystal until she eats some."

Zoey went to the pitcher of lemonade and

filled paper cups for Tanya and herself, then headed back into the living room where everyone was sitting. Dane stood behind a vacant chair. After passing a cup to Tanya on the couch, Zoey took the seat in front of Dane, amazed he was still wearing his new suit. He looked uncomfortable in the buttoned-up shirt with a tie, which surprised her because he had always worn a suit when he had gone into the office in Dallas. But then she guessed she shouldn't be surprised because for the past few years, he hadn't worn one.

She twisted around and smiled up at Dane. "There's a lot of food in the kitchen."

"Not hungry." He clasped the back of the chair and stared at James Norton, following intently what the man was saying to Tanya.

The stiffness in Norton's bearing and the stilted sound to his words accentuated the man's uneasiness. This was a duty call, nothing more, Dane thought, taking in the slender man's pinched features. Immaculately dressed even down to his black polished shoes, Norton appeared every inch old money who had deemed it necessary to visit an employee out of a sense of obligation because he was the president of the bank. Not because he cared.

When Nick slid into the chair near Norton, the man quickly averted his attention from Tanya to speak with Nick, who Dane was sure was a large depositor at the bank. Frowning, Dane ran his finger along the side of his collar, the material too tight around the neck. Since his disappearance he hadn't worn a suit except once on his date with Zoey and its constriction stunned him. When had that changed? He'd never thought twice about it before his disappearance.

The ringing of the phone startled him out of his musing.

Beth, who had answered it for Tanya, said, "Dane, it's for you."

"You can take it in the kitchen if you want," Tanya said from the couch, appearing out of place next to Norton.

In the kitchen, Dane lifted the wall receiver and said, "Hello."

"Mr. Witherspoon, it's Eddy. You need to get home *now*."

The urgency in the teen's voice made Dane grip the phone even tighter. "Why? Where are you?"

"Just get home. Someone's breaking into your house."

Dane quickly hung up and strode toward the

back door. Outside on the deck he called to Jesse, "Tell Zoey I had to go home. I'll come back later and pick her up."

He hurried away so fast he didn't hear what Jesse said in reply. He focused all his thoughts on getting home in time to stop whatever was going down. He suspected it was Clark and his friends. How else would Eddy know?

A few minutes later he pulled up to the curb in front of Wilbur's house. He surveyed his home and couldn't see anything out of place even though the sun was almost down behind the tall oaks across the street. He slipped his cell phone out of his pocket and ran through the neighbors' yards toward the back of his house.

A broken window and a door ajar alerted him to danger lurking inside. He flipped open his phone and punched in the police's number. After reporting the break-in, he pocketed the cell and weaved his way toward the deck. Plastering himself up flat against his house, he listened, wishing he had his gun, which to his horror was stored on the top shelf of the closet in the hallway. He hoped the intruders didn't find it and the ammo and that they didn't have one with them.

The sound of something crashing to the floor

stiffened him. Dane leaned as close to the broken window as he could and not be detected. Male voices floated to him, boiling his anger.

"He'll regret the day he messed with me," came the declaration followed by the ripping of fabric.

Clark Norton! Dane saw red, his hands fisting at his sides. He should wait for backup, but if he did, his home would be destroyed by the punks. He eased the back door open and crept over the threshold.

"This is for turning me in to the police," the young male voice said.

All around Dane lay broken pieces of their dishes and containers of food torn open and dumped on the tile floor, as though a bomb had been detonated in his kitchen. Fury welled up, and Dane had to force it down in order to remain in control.

Glass shattered. The noise coming from the living room drove him to tap into all his training that had laid dormant for nearly three years. The intruders were at the front of the house, having a good ol' time from the sounds of their destruction. If he could get to the hall closet off the kitchen and retrieve his gun, then hopefully he could put an end to this senselessness.

He picked his way through the remnants of

the teenagers' rage and eased the door to the hallway open, peering out into the corridor. Empty. The continual havoc being waged on his home resonated through it. Again he had to tap into his determination to stay in control to keep himself from storming down the hall to stop the punks.

He edged toward the closet, flipping on the light switch. Inching the door open, he slid inside. After finding his gun in its locked box on the top shelf in the back, he hunted for the ammunition, kept in a separate area, and loaded his weapon, then slipped back out into the hallway.

"We'd better leave, Clark. We've been here longer than we usually stay."

Dane flattened himself against the wall near the entrance into the living room. Bringing his gun up, he readied himself to step forward.

"One more room. The den, then we're out of here. They're all at Crystal's. Can't believe so many turned out for the funeral of a criminal."

The sound of the male voices grew nearer. Dane saw Clark first, then another boy coming into the entry hall. He knew there were three but the last one must have hung back. If Dane didn't do something soon, Clark and his friend would spot him.

Dane waited for a second, hoping the third one would appear. When he didn't, he made his move, bracing himself with his feet apart, his weapon leveled at the two. Out of the corner of his eye, Dane glimpsed the third teen, still in the living room, off to the side.

"Stop right there," Dane said in his toughest voice.

Clark and the second boy whirled around and froze while the third one ducked back behind the living room entrance. Dane heard the pounding of the fleeing teen as he ran toward the kitchen and out the back door.

"It seems your friend has left you," Dane said, his gaze never leaving the two punks in his entryway.

The teen next to Clark shook, a look of fear gripping him, while Clark straightened to his full height, disdain in his expression.

"What are ya gonna do? Shoot us?" Clark took a step back toward the front door, then another one.

"So you think if you run, I won't do anything. You broke into my house. I don't have to shoot to kill. I can wound you so you won't be going anywhere. Is that what you want? 'Cause if it is, then keep taking a step back."

Clark stopped, his glare lethal, a tic pulsating in his jaw.

Dane saw the flashing red lights out the window next to the front door.

The second boy's eyes widened. "The police, Clark!"

Clark glanced behind him, but when he turned back, none of the insolence was gone. "So? This is no big deal. We'll be free by this evening."

Dane gritted his teeth and waited for Zach to arrive. He'd seen people like Clark before. They thought they were above the law. He would soon find out he wasn't, but the damage they had done would still be here. The only satisfaction Dane had was that hopefully Clark's terror in Sweetwater would come to an end. He was pretty sure he had been trying to get Eddy involved, using strong-arm tactics, and he had a strong feeling these teens had been behind the recent robbery spree.

Dane motioned to the two to move to the side so he could open the front door. For a few seconds Clark stood his ground, his glare drilling hatred into Dane, before the other tugged his cohort to the side. Dane let Zach and another officer into his house.

"We caught Joey fleeing from your backyard.

My other officer has him in the car already. So what happened here?" Zach asked, removing his handcuffs.

Dane dropped his gun as Zach snapped the cuffs on Clark, then the other teen. "Breaking and entering. Destroying property. I *will* be pressing charges." He motioned toward the living room.

Zach whistled. "They really did a number."

"'Fraid so."

"What do you boys have to say for yourself?"

"I want a lawyer," Clark said.

"Read them their rights and take them down to the station. I'll be along in a minute," Zach said to the officer with him.

After they left, Dane relaxed his tensed body, pocketing the gun. "You know, I think they have been the ones robbing the houses."

"Yep. I bet you're right, but I don't know if we'll be able to prove that. I'm hoping we can get one of the teens to turn on the others."

"Clark has to be the leader."

"I agree. I'll see what Joey and Adam have to say first. Let Clark sweat a little." Zach started to leave but stopped. "One of my officers is retiring next month. We sure could use someone like you on the force if you ever decide to leave the DEA. I know it wouldn't be the excitement you're used to, but this job is fulfilling."

Dane smiled. "Thanks. I'll think about it."

As Zach left, Dane was surprised that he was tempted by the job offer. He'd never thought of himself as a police officer, but it could be an answer for him. Would the job fulfill him? Would it help erase the guilt that ate at him?

He sank down on the second stair, exhausted by the past half hour's activity and the long day with Tom's funeral. He'd seen firsthand today the sorrow a death wielded on a family. That was what had happened to his when they had thought he had died in the plane crash.

Burying his face in his hands, he tried to wipe the picture from his thoughts of Crystal sobbing at the graveside, of Tanya trying to comfort her daughter and barely holding herself together. The sounds echoed through his mind. Zoey had gone through something similar because of him.

"What happened here?"

Dane jerked his head up and found Zoey with Tara in her arms standing in the doorway of the house. Blake and Mandy, eyes saucer-round, were next to her. He shoved to his feet and quickly covered the distance between him and his family.

"Three teens vandalized our home," Dane said as he took Tara from Zoey and held her close to him, needing the feel of his youngest in his arms. So innocent—untouched by ugly realities in the world. But it wasn't enough to solve his problems. He drew the rest of his family to him, holding them for a long moment, relishing the lavender scent of Zoey's perfume, such a familiar smell that always managed to soothe.

Zoey pulled back. "Who would do this?"

While Blake walked toward the living room with Mandy right behind him, Dane said, "Clark Norton, Joey and Adam. I don't know their last names. Blake, Mandy, be careful."

His son stopped at the entrance, holding his sister back. "Everything's smashed."

"Daddy, our pictures are broken."

With Tara still cuddled against him, Dane came up to Mandy and placed one hand on her shoulder. "We'll get everything fixed, especially the pictures, princess."

"Why'd they do this, Daddy?"

"A good question. I'm not sure. I think they weren't happy I told the police about them speeding the other night."

Mandy turned her big, brown eyes up at him. "Didya catch them?"

He nodded. "The police took them away. We'll be safe, so don't you worry."

Blake balled his hands. "I bet it was Joey Miller. He's always with Clark. I know his younger brother. I should——"

Dane passed Tara to Zoey, then clasped his son by the shoulders so he would look at him. "Joey's brother had nothing to do with this. Retaliation of any sort isn't what Christ taught us."

"No, but——"

"There are no buts, son. Do I make myself clear?"

Blake dropped his gaze. "Yes, sir."

"Good. Now I believe it's nearing Mandy and Tara's bedtime. Why don't you help me clean up, Blake, while Mom puts the girls down?"

Blake's expression brightened. "Sure."

"I want to help," Mandy said with a pout.

"You can tomorrow," Zoey said, leading his daughters toward the stairs.

"Tomorrow's a school day. You'd better go on to bed," Dane said, righting another chair in the kitchen.

Blake tried to stifle a yawn, but he couldn't

quite. "I'll help tomorrow when I get home from school, Dad."

"Good night and thanks, son."

As Blake darted from the room, Zoey entered, taking a look at the mess still covering the counters and floor. "They must have been in here a while to do this kind of damage."

"I don't think so. It doesn't take long to rip, tear and shatter."

"I've known Joey for several years and Adam, too. I don't understand this." She swept her arm across her body.

"I think Clark is very good at manipulating people. Peer pressure can be tough, but you know that."

"How did you know about them?"

"Eddy called and told me to get home."

Zoey went to the closet and withdrew the broom and dustpan. "He wasn't involved, was he?"

"No, but I think he's been watching our house. Guarding it, so to speak."

She paused in her sweeping and looked at Dane. "So he knew something would happen?"

"Yes. I think he's suspected they have been robbing the houses in town. He maybe even knew for sure but was too scared to say anything."

"They did push him out of a moving truck."

"He probably told them no, and I get the feeling Clark doesn't like the word no."

Zoey began sweeping up the flour and sugar with shards of glass and ceramic mixed in. "I need to thank Eddy when I see him."

Dane took the dustpan and held it for her. "Just don't let anyone know he called me. I don't want them or their friends retaliating against him."

"That took courage for Eddy to stand up to them."

"Yeah. I want to help him deal with his dad's drinking."

"Do you think he'll listen to you?"

Dane dumped the contents of the dustpan into the garbage can. "I hope so, since I speak from experience."

Zoey nearly dropped the broom she was holding. "Your dad was an alcoholic?" She shifted her gaze to Dane who watched her.

"Yes. At the end he drank all the time."

"Why haven't you ever said anything about that?"

"There wasn't any reason. You don't drink. I don't drink."

This time she did release the broom, its crash

against the floor loud in the sudden silence. She stepped toward Dane. "That had to have been important to you as you were growing up. Why wouldn't you think I would want to know that?"

He tore his gaze away from hers and twisted around to start cleaning up the mess on the counter.

She reached around him and stopped his movements. "I told you about my father's unexpected death from an accident at work. I told you about my struggle to understand it. I told you everything about me. The joys, the disappointments."

Edging away, he turned toward her, his unreadable mask in place. "It's the past. I like to leave the past in the past. What can I or, for that matter, you do about it now?"

"I can't change the past, but I can support you. What happened in your past molds who you are today. It helps me understand you better. Don't you understand it connects us when we share our feelings?"

"I felt helpless. I couldn't change what was happening. I couldn't help my dad. I—" Dane closed his eyes, pain carved into his expression. "I tried, but nothing I did changed his drinking."

"He had to want to change."

"I know that now. But the bottom line is that

my brother and I weren't enough reason for him to change."

The anguish in his gaze pierced through her heart. "Addiction, in whatever form, is extremely hard to overcome. Some people aren't strong enough to break the chains."

"Eddy's father may never, but I want to help him understand. I didn't have anyone when I was going through it. I don't want that to happen with Eddy. When the youth center gets going, this is something that can be dealt with there. Support groups for kids, dealing with different issues."

"Then why don't you head up the center?"

Horror flitted across his face. He backed away. "I can't! All I know is how to be a DEA agent. Don't make me into something I'm not." Dane pivoted and strode toward the back door.

Zoey watched him leave. She had glimpsed some of the pain he'd endured as a child, but she sensed something else driving him besides his father's drinking problem. He'd opened the door into his heart and given her a peek at who he truly was, then slammed it closed. It was a start. But would they have enough time to really connect before he went back to work for the DEA and fell into his old patterns?

## Chapter Eleven

"We stopped at Tanya's on the way over here," Beth said, stepping inside Zoey's house with Samuel and their kids following.

"How's she doing?" Zoey asked, taking the cake Beth had baked for dessert.

"Dealing. In a lot of ways she'd already said goodbye to Tom when he divorced her. It's Crystal who's having a hard time."

"Craig and Allie, Mandy and Blake are out back with Dane." Zoey led the way into the kitchen and waited until the two children went outside before saying, "I think she blames herself for her father being in prison."

"I suspected that," Samuel said, heading for the back door. "I've tried talking to her, but she just clams up."

"I know how that can be. Blake did the same thing. Thankfully he finally spoke up with Dane."

After her husband left, Beth said, "I'm finding more reasons every day for the center. Samuel says they're going to start next week, gutting the inside of the building, making sure it's sound."

"I think this summer will be spent working on it. It'll give us and the kids a project."

"Samuel's already organizing the other churches. Recruiting the youth groups to help. He wants the kids to feel they have a part in making this center happen."

"That's great." Zoey pulled the platter of hamburger patties from the refrigerator. "We're gonna eat out back. It's a perfect Saturday night for a picnic. No rain in sight. Seventy-five degrees."

"Can I help with anything?"

"Nope. I've got everything under control. The table's already set on the deck. Let's join the guys." Zoey walked to the door, letting Pepper out back at the same time.

Outside she paused, taking in the kids playing in the yard, the cat trotting up to Mandy and weaving in and out of her legs while her daughter giggled. Blake and Craig were dribbling and passing the soccer ball. Mandy, Allie and Tara were playing by the playhouse. Dane, laughing at something Samuel had said, was by the grill, getting it started. The scene before her made her throat constrict with emotions. If only this could be captured in a bottle to be released again and again. But next week Dane would leave for Dallas and everything could change after that trip.

"Are you all right?" Beth asked.

"Just relishing the moment."

"Yeah, I know what you mean. No one's arguing. Everyone's getting along."

"Speaking of family, where's Jane?"

"On a date."

"How's Samuel doing?"

"Trying not to think about it. She just started dating, and he paces the whole time she's gone."

"We have a few years until Mandy starts—thankfully. I think Dane will be worse." Zoey started toward the men by the grill. "I haven't seen Jane in my office much this year."

"This was a very good year for her. I'm so proud of her."

"Well, she's got you at school."

Beth smiled, her whole face lighting up. "That

she does. It's nice to be able to help her right away if there's a problem with one of her classes. But I haven't had to do much lately. She's really throwing herself into her school work."

"Good, now if I could only get Blake to see the value of doing homework."

"You, too? Craig and I battle every night over that."

"Battle over what?" Samuel asked.

"Homework. He told me the other night he thought he would be a rock star or a pro soccer player so he didn't need to do homework."

Dane took the platter from Zoey. "I think he and Blake have been talking. That's what Blake has decided to be."

"Maybe I shouldn't have asked their band to play at church?" Samuel shifted around to peer at the boys in the yard.

"No, ignoring their talents isn't the answer. Hopefully something else will click into place as they go through high school. I've seen it with other kids." Zoey leaned back against the railing. "Are they gonna play?"

"They're working on it. I think they will during the summer."

"That'll be their first engagement," Beth said, taking a seat on a lounge chair nearby.

"I can't believe Blake didn't say anything to us." Dane placed the hamburgers on the grill.

"He probably wanted to surprise you. We're looking at the first Sunday after school is out."

"I can't believe, Samuel Morgan, you didn't say anything to me." Beth sent a stern look toward her husband.

"Actually it slipped my mind with all that's been happening lately."

"Yeah, Tom's death, the break-ins, the arrest of the three boys." Zoey moved to the love seat across from Beth, stunned at all that had been happening in Sweetwater when she thought back over the past few months. The one thing that had impacted her life the most she hadn't even listed—Dane's return.

"The robberies should stop now since Joey confessed it was them." Dane flipped the patties over. "I was worried that Clark would get away with them, but that doesn't look like that will be the case. Since Clark's seventeen, they're looking at trying him as an adult. It seems this isn't the first time he's been in trouble with the law. He had trouble with the police where he lived before Sweetwater. His father's influence got him out of it the last time, but I don't think it'll work this time."

"What's so sad was that Joey and Adam were dragged into his schemes. I don't want something like that to happen again in Sweetwater." Samuel sat on the end of Beth's lounge chair, taking her hand.

Turning from the grill, Dane said, "You know, I've been thinking about the center. What if we have a youth board to help run the place?"

Samuel cocked his head to the side and thought a moment. "I like that. There would have to be adult supervision, but it would give the kids a say in how the center is run."

"Watch out!" Blake yelled right before the soccer ball landed in the middle of them. He ran up to the deck and grabbed it. "Sorry. We're practicing headers."

"If you want, after dinner I'll help you and Craig." Dane began removing the hamburgers from the fire. "But right now it's time to eat."

"Blake, get your sisters. Allie and Craig and you all go in and wash your hands." Zoey stood to go into the kitchen to bring out the rest of the food.

"I'll help," Beth said, scurrying after Zoey.

Inside Zoey withdrew the potato salad and coleslaw from the refrigerator. The kids ran through the kitchen.

"Where are they going?" Beth asked, loading a tray with ketchup, mustard, tomatoes, lettuce and pickles for the hamburgers.

"To the bathroom."

"But there's a sink right here."

"And we're right here. This way I don't supervise their less-than-satisfactory method of hand-washing."

Beth planted herself in the entrance of the kitchen and forced each one of the children to show her his hands. Mandy and Craig had to go back and redo theirs.

"I knew there was a reason we're good friends," Zoey said with a laugh. "We think alike."

"I didn't want to say anything outside, but—" Beth walked back to the counter to get her tray "—the discussion earlier only confirms in my mind that Dane should head the center. He'd be perfect, especially since he's had training as a counselor. Is there anyway we can convince him to take the job?"

"I wish. It would be an answer to one of my prayers." Zoey lifted first one bowl, then balanced the other on top of it. "I've never really understood why he walked away from counseling all those years ago. As usual, my husband is silent on that. If I knew, then maybe I could help."

"Some people think they can do everything by themselves, but I learned I couldn't without the Lord's help. Maybe Dane will turn to God to guide him."

"He's going to church, which is something I didn't think I would see. Tomorrow he's even going by Eddy's to pick him up."

"Good. Eddy has missed attending lately. Do you know what's going on with the boy?"

Zoey nodded, managing to open the back door. "But it's not something I can share. Dane's determined to help Eddy and maybe in the process the teen can help my husband."

Beth sent her a quizzical look.

"It'll get Dane involved in Sweetwater. He says we won't return to Dallas, that he'll relocate in Kentucky with the DEA, but I'm afraid his wishes won't prevail. What will I do if I have to choose whether to uproot my family to return to what I had once? I can't live that life again."

Beth stepped out onto the deck. "I'll pray for you. I wish I could do more."

"That's enough. Thanks, Beth." Zoey crossed to the table set for dinner and put the bowls in the center as Dane brought the platter of hamburgers.

For a few seconds Zoey stood back and

watched as the children scrambled for their seats, laughter and the scent of grilled meat filling the air. Dane's gleaming gaze caught hold of hers and her heart skipped a beat. His mouth cocked up in a lopsided grin and warmth flowed through her. Family and friends. What could be better than this? She wanted to freeze this moment in time to cherish later when Dane left for Dallas. Lonely days followed by even lonelier nights were ahead.

Sunday morning Dane picked up the phone on the second ring. "Hello." He looked toward Zoey, who was cleaning up the breakfast dishes, her beauty growing each day he was with her.

"Mr. Witherspoon, this is Eddy."

Dane became alert, his hand grasping the receiver tightly. "Yes?" He could tell something was wrong by the sound in the boy's voice.

"I can't get my dad up."

"I'll be right over." Dane replaced the phone and snatched up the car keys. "I've got to go over to Eddy's. Something's wrong. I'll call you when I know something?"

"I'll come with you. Blake can watch—" Zoey's face fell. "No, he's at Craig's. I can't leave Tara and Mandy by themselves."

Dane yanked open the back door. "I know. I'll call."

As he drove to Eddy's, Dane kept going over in his mind images of him and his dad. His father had been a mean drunk. Thankfully, though, he'd usually drink so much that he passed out after only an hour or so. He could remember trying to wake his dad once, and when he couldn't, how scared he'd become. His neighbor had come over and finally helped arouse his father from his drunken stupor. But the fear had planted itself every time after that when his dad started drinking until he lost consciousness. Would he wake up this time? What would he and Jacob do if they lost their father, too? But the worse thought had been when he and his brother were hiding from their father until he passed out, the wish that he would lose consciousness so Jacob and he would be safe for another night.

Dane pulled up into the driveway and rushed up to the front porch. Before he had a chance to knock, Eddy opened the door, worry etched deep into his features.

"I still can't get him up. What do I do?"

"Let me try a few things. If they don't work, we'll need to call 911."

"911!" Eddy's eyes grew round, fear chasing away the worry.

Dane had been there and knew what Eddy was experiencing. He wished he could take it away, but he also knew that he couldn't. Eddy would always worry about his father and fear that one day he wouldn't wake up from passing out.

Dane trailed after Eddy to the den where the smell of alcohol overpowered him, churning his stomach. That very scent always produced that reaction in him.

Dane pulled the man up from the couch and shook him. "Keith, wake up. Keith!"

The man's head lolled to the side, his body limp.

"See, Mr. Witherspoon?"

Dane laid him back on the cushion, one of his arms dropping to the floor. "I'll be right back."

Dane went into the kitchen and got a glass of cold water, then headed back to the den. "Stand back." Pouring it onto Keith's face, he readied himself for the man to come up, startled and possibly hostile.

Groaning, Eddy's father batted at an invisible person. Water dripped off him, wetting the cushion and his stained white T-shirt. Dane reached for the man again and brought him up.

Getting into the man's face, Dane yelled, "Get up, Keith! Now!"

Keith's eyes blinked open as he struggled to get loose of Dane's grip. "What the—" The man's mouth dropped, his gaze glued to Dane.

Dane released Eddy's father, who fell back against the couch. "Your son was worried when he couldn't get you up." Dane glanced at the teen and said, "Go put some coffee on, Eddy, and bring me a large glass of water."

"I'm up. I'm up. You—don't—need—" Keith struggled to push himself to a sitting position.

"You need to drink some water, dilute some of the liquor in your system," Dane said as the boy left the room. "Now while Eddy is gone, I have a few things to say to you. You have a choice, Keith. You can either continue to drink and probably kill yourself or someone else in the process, or you can get help. Do you have any idea what you're doing to your son? He covers for you and tries to take care of you. He isn't the parent in this situation, but you're forcing him to be. He needs you. He's been in trouble and I doubt you know anything about it."

"Trou-ble? Ed-dy?" Keith labored over each syllable. "I don't—under-stand."

"Didn't you wonder how Eddy hurt himself

a week ago? Or, did you even notice?" The man's frown prompted Dane to add, "Your son was thrown from a moving truck by some boys who've been trying to get him to do things that are illegal."

Keith slowly swung his legs to the floor, dropped his head into his hands and groaned. "I didn't know."

"That's not a surprise. I doubt you've been aware of anything going on lately."

Keith's shoulders hunched even more as if the man was trying to curl into a tight ball. "I can't—think."

"Your son needs help from his father, not added problems. So what are you gonna do about this?" Dane glared down at Keith, his hands flexed at his sides, his body taut with tension. In his mind he saw his dad when he'd aroused himself from a drunken stupor. He'd been all contrite, apologizing for his behavior until the next time.

Eddy's father lifted his head and looked at Dane. "I don't know what to do."

"You can start by going to AA. There's a group that meets at Sweetwater Community Church on Monday nights. You need help. It's hard to lick this problem without it. But you have to want that help or it won't work."

"I'll think—" The sound of Eddy's footsteps approaching silenced Keith's reply.

Dane leaned close and whispered, "Think long and hard what you want to be for your son."

"I've got the coffee on. Here's the water, Dad."

Keith wrinkled his nose as though the liquid were offensive to him.

"Drink it, Keith."

The man took the glass Eddy held out and sipped the liquid. The scent of coffee brewing permeated the room, tangling with the smells of alcohol. Keith finally finished the water and set the glass down on the table next to the couch.

"Mr. Witherspoon, I'd better not go with you to church this morning."

Keith struggled to his feet, paused a few seconds to get his bearing, then started for the kitchen. "Son, go. I'll be okay. I'm gonna drink that whole pot of coffee, then clean up."

"But, Dad, you—"

Keith turned in the entrance into the kitchen and said, "What I need is to see you attending church again." He shuffled toward the stove where the coffeepot was. "Mr. Witherspoon, please take him."

Dane nodded.

Eddy stared at his father for a long moment,

watching him pour a mug full of the hot brew then ease down at the table to drink his coffee, slouching over the wooden surface. "Okay, Dad, if you're sure."

His father waved him away. "I'm sure."

Eddy darted for the door, saying, "I can get ready in five minutes."

The sound of his footsteps pounding up the stairs echoed through the house. Keith winced at the noise and brought the mug to his lips.

"Want any?" the man asked between sips.

"No, thanks. All I want is for you to go to the AA meeting. At least check it out. Your son needs you sober."

"He's got you," Keith mumbled into the mug.

"No one can replace a father in a boy's life."

Keith shifted his bloodshot gaze to Dane. "You sound like you speak from experience."

Relieved to hear Eddy coming down the stairs, Dane didn't answer the man. "I'll bring your son home after church. That should give you time to clean yourself up."

Frowning, Keith drank some more of his coffee and looked down as though the surface of the table was the most interesting object he had seen.

Dane met Eddy at the entrance into the kitchen. "We need to go and pick up my family."

Outside on the porch Dane took a deep breath of fresh air, the churning in his stomach settling down. The smell had brought back bad memories of dealing with his own father. His heart went out to Eddy and he hoped he could be there for the teen, even if his dad wasn't.

"Do you think he'll be okay?" Eddy asked as they walked toward the minivan.

"Yes." He'd seen it with his own father. Remorse would last a while, then the drinking pattern would start all over—unless Keith got help.

Eddy climbed into the passenger seat. "I don't know. Dad was really upset about something at work."

"He has to figure out on his own that drinking won't solve the problem, that it'll actually make it worse."

"How?"

"I suggested he go to AA at the church on Monday night."

Eddy shook his head. "He won't. He doesn't want anyone to know. That's why he drinks at home, not at bars. I think he's afraid he'll lose his job."

"People know. They always find out eventually, especially in a small town." Dane backed out of the driveway and headed toward his house.

"Except for you and your wife, I haven't told a soul."

"When a person has a drinking problem, it starts showing up in other areas of their life. You said yourself that he didn't go to work for a few days a couple of weeks ago because of the drinking."

"How do you know so much?"

"Because I've been there with my own dad." The words came out slowly. They had been buried deep inside for so long, but as with Zoey, telling Eddy felt right.

"He drank?"

"Yes, every night when he would get home from work for years. And like you, I didn't know what to do about it. I wanted to help him, but he wouldn't let me. I felt so helpless watching my dad kill himself with each drink he downed."

"Is he alive?"

"No, he died from a heart attack."

"He wouldn't go to AA?"

"Nope. Didn't think he had a problem."

"Do you think Dad will go?"

Dane glanced at Eddy. "I don't know. I hope so."

"What do I do if he doesn't?"

"Get help for yourself."

"But I don't have the problem."

"You're living with an alcoholic. That's a problem you'll need to learn to deal with. There are groups to support the family members of an alcoholic. Join one even if your father doesn't go to AA."

"I'll think about it."

Dane parked in his driveway and twisted toward Eddy. "You need to take care of yourself, but you aren't alone. I'll help anyway I can."

"Why do you care?"

"Because no one helped me. I don't want you to go through what I did." He thought of the people in his town who had turned a blind eye to what was happening in his life. He wasn't going to let that happen to Eddy.

The teen lowered his gaze, fidgeting with the handle. "Thanks for not telling anyone I warned you about the break-in."

"I did tell my wife, but she won't say anything. I don't want there to be any problems because you did."

"I haven't seen Clark since he was taken in. Do you think he'll figure it out?"

"He thinks I just came home early. There isn't

any reason for him to think otherwise. He's more concerned about Joey and Adam's confessions."

Zoey and the children appeared on the porch. Mandy raced toward the van while his wife locked the front door. Blake took Tara's hand and walked her out to the vehicle with Zoey following.

"I don't understand how Joey and Adam let Clark talk them into robbing those houses. They've always been a bit wild, but they've never done anything like that." Eddy climbed out and moved to the backseat while the children piled into the vehicle.

When Zoey was settled in the front, Dane said, "You'll find, Eddy, in life there are leaders and there are followers. Joey and Adam are followers who didn't use good judgment on who to follow. What you have to decide is what type of person you want to be, a leader or a follower."

"Daddy, I like to play follow the leader." Mandy squirmed in the seat between Blake and Eddy.

"That's a fun game. Maybe we can play it when we get home from church." Dane slid a look toward Zoey.

Her smile warmed him, chasing away some of the coldness about his heart. While Blake asked Eddy a question about high school, Dane slipped his hand toward Zoey's and squeezed it. The connection made the painful memories fade. She'd always been his ray of hope in a world filled with ugliness. But had he ever given her what she needed? He was afraid of that answer.

## *Chapter Twelve*

Her face flushed, Zoey rushed into the house, the back door slamming shut behind her. "Sorry, I'm late. Mom started talking and time just slipped away. I'll be dressed in five minutes."

Dane watched his wife, not breaking a stride, hurry out of the kitchen. He finished drinking his fifth cup of coffee that day and put the mug into the sink. This time tomorrow he would be in Dallas, trying to decide what to do with his life, his career. And he didn't have an answer.

Tonight Zoey had arranged for her mother to take care of Tara while Mandy was at dance class and Blake was practicing at the Morgans'. They were finally going to jog together after juggling theirs and the kids' schedules. How had Zoey kept up with everything by herself?

The doorbell chimed. Dane strode toward the entry hall, shouting upstairs, "I'll get it."

Surprise rippled through him when he saw Eddy on his front porch. "Is everything okay?"

A smile transformed the teenager's face. "Yes! I know you're leaving for Dallas tomorrow morning, but I wanted to let you know my dad went to the AA meeting last night."

The hope and enthusiasm in Eddy's voice spurred Dane's. "That's great! What did he think?"

"He's gonna go back next week. And he wants me to go to the meeting for the family members."

"That'll be good for you. I hope you do."

"This wouldn't have been possible if you hadn't helped me. I wanted to thank you before you left." Eddy stuck out his hand.

Dane shook it, his throat tightening. "I'll be back. I'm only going for a few days, so we can talk some more this weekend. Do you want us to pick you up for church?"

"No, Dad and I are gonna go this Sunday. Dad came home tonight from work all excited. Mr. Norton has announced he'll be leaving the bank and Sweetwater at the end of the summer, which will make things a whole lot more comfortable for me and Dad."

"I can see how that will be better for everyone." Dane hoped that this burst of fervor from Eddy's father would last past his first disappointment. He wished he could be here for the teen in case his dad had a relapse. Having gone through several with his own while growing up, he knew what Eddy would experience when he discovered his father drinking again. Perhaps it wouldn't happen, but still he wanted to be around for Eddy in case it did.

"Hi, Mrs. Witherspoon," Eddy said, looking behind Dane.

Dane turned toward Zoey. "Eddy's dad went to the AA meeting last night at the church."

Zoey smiled as she finished putting her hair up into a ponytail. "That's wonderful."

"Well, I'd better be going. It looks like you two are gonna go running."

"I'm going to try to keep up with my husband. I'm out of practice."

"Mr. Witherspoon, you'll have to slow your pace."

Dane chuckled. "Are you kidding, Eddy? She can run circles around me."

When Eddy left, Zoey playfully punched Dane in the arm. "You're exaggerating, Dane

Witherspoon. I haven't gotten a chance to run in a month."

Dane raised both his brows. "Maybe we should race then."

"Sure. Better get the key and lock the door." Zoey stepped out onto the porch.

While he went to the table in the entryway where he kept his keys, Zoey spun around, leaped off the porch and started running.

"Hey, you cheated," she heard Dane shout behind her.

At the street Zoey turned around and jogged backwards. "A gal's gotta do what she's gotta do."

Moving forward again, Zoey concentrated on putting some distance between her and Dane. She hadn't jogged much since Dane's return, but before that she had a lot. Thankfully her body fell into its old rhythm. Several blocks away from the house, she glanced back and saw that Dane was keeping up but hadn't gained any on her. Again focusing forward, she settled into a comfortable pace, her breathing even.

Two more blocks and Zoey thought maybe she should slow down. After all she should be running *with* Dane, not from him. She peered over her shoulder to see how far back he was. The street was empty!

Her pace faltered. Cutting her speed in half, she tried to determined what had happened to Dane. What if he'd tripped or hurt himself? She came to a stop, contemplating what to do when suddenly from behind someone tackled her to the grass on the side of the road.

For a split second her heart seemed to cease beating until she felt the familiar arms of her husband pinning her to the ground and smelled his particular masculine scent mingling with earthy odors of dirt and grass.

He leaned close to her ear, her cheek pressed into the green softness. "If you can start without me, I can take a shortcut to even the playing field."

The tickle of his breath along her neck sent a shiver down her. The warmth of his body covering hers produced visions of intimate nights spent in his embrace—an eternity ago.

He shoved himself up, sitting on the lawn, his arms resting on his raised knees. Zoey rolled over and looked up at her husband. The proud angle of his profile, the way the fading sunlight highlighted the strands of silver in his dark hair, caught her full attention. Now her heart pounded a quick tempo that had nothing to do with her jog. Would their relationship ever get back to the way it had been when they had first married—when life and work hadn't intruded into their world?

Zoey pushed to a sitting position next to Dane, her arm brushing up against his. Noticing they were on Beth and Samuel's front lawn with the church next door, she said, "Do you want to go see how Blake is doing?"

Dane shook his head. "This is our time. Besides, I want to be surprised when he plays at church for the first time."

"So you're gonna continue to attend church?" She held her breath waiting for his answer.

"Yes. Samuel's inspiring and a good friend. I've never had time to form friendships before because of my work."

"But what about God?"

He quirked a brow. "What about Him?"

"That's what church is all about. Do you believe or are you just going to please me?"

"Honestly I'm still trying to figure that one out. When I was growing up, I went to church when my mother was alive. Dad couldn't be bothered. After she died, I tried to go with a friend, but it became increasingly hard. Then when I sought God's help, my prayers were never answered. I stopped praying and relied only on myself."

"Have you ever considered that was the Lord's answer? That He wanted you to be strong, capable of dealing with your father's drinking?"

His eyes darkened. "It's not that simple." Climbing to his feet, Dane started toward the church.

Zoey caught up with him near the entrance into the Garden of Serenity. "I never said it was simple. Life is anything but that. But loving God *is* simple. You put your trust in the Lord to be there for you in the bad and good times as your support. It doesn't mean that life's problems go away. It just means you aren't alone in dealing with them."

"How do you turn control over to Him?"

"That's easy. He only has your best interest in His heart."

Dane paced back and forth in front of the pond. "I had to learn early I was the only one I could depend on."

Zoey clasped his arm, stopping him. "It doesn't have to be that way. I'm here for you. God's here for you."

"I'm thirty-eight years old. How do I change

a lifetime habit?" He shrugged out of her grasp and put some distance between them.

His gesture pierced her heart as though he were stating that she and their love were not enough for him. "One step at a time. But first you have to want to change." *Let me in. Let me help you.*

Dane watched the play of emotions flicker into her eyes with a silent plea finally settling over her features. *How do I let go of the past? It's what made me who I am today.* He'd tried to ignore the memories, but they always seeped through to haunt him when he least expected them. "I don't—" He couldn't voice aloud his failures. He wanted to tell her, had told her more than anyone else, but he'd bore his guilt alone for so long he didn't know how to change that.

Zoey's expression crumbled, hurt in her eyes. She whirled around and jogged toward the entrance. Dane started to go after her, then realized he couldn't reassure her. He couldn't give her what she wanted—to lay his soul bare for her. Their marriage was on such a rocky foundation he didn't want to see disgust or pity in her eyes.

Dane sank down on the bench, clasped his hands and stared at the ground. *Lord, Zoey says*

*You're here to help. If that's so, I need it. My life's a mess. How do I fix it?*

Long minutes passed but no answer came to mind. The sun sank below the trees. Shadows fingered their way through the garden. What had he expected—a declaration blasted from the heavens?

"Dane?"

He looked up to see Samuel standing by the pond.

"I didn't realize you were here."

"Yeah, just thinking."

"This place's good for that." Samuel took a seat on the bench opposite Dane. "Concerned about your trip to Dallas?"

"I wish it were that simple."

"Eddy came by a little while ago. He ended up helping the boys with their band. They were so excited about getting help from a high-schooler."

"His dad's getting help finally."

"I know. Eddy told me. He is, too. It might not have happened without your intervention."

Dane lifted his shoulder in a shrug. "Someone else would have stepped in."

"You're selling yourself short. You're the one who turned Eddy around."

Dane peered away, following the progress of the goldfish as they swam in the pool.

"Do you want to tell me what's bothering you?"

Samuel's question came to him as though his friend had spoken through a long tunnel. Dane remembered the hurt in Zoey's eyes as she had spun away and fled the garden. "How do you get rid of guilt?"

"Have you truly confronted the problem? Have you turned it over to the Lord?"

Dane snorted. "It's not that simple."

"I didn't say it was simple. It isn't." Samuel leaned forward, resting his elbows on his thighs. "But if you keep it bottled up inside of you, it will eat at you until there's nothing left. I know. I did the same thing. When my first wife died, I felt guilty for surviving without her. She was my whole life, or so I had thought. It took God and Beth to show me there was more to my life, that I still had a lot to give."

Dane didn't know what to say to his friend. His emotions were so jumbled, as though they were a ball of yarn that couldn't be unraveled.

Samuel rose. "You've done a lot for the people of Sweetwater in the short time you've been here. Because of you, we'll be getting a

much-needed youth center. And you personally touched a young man who desperately
needed help. There comes a time you have to
let go of your past, to turn it over to the Lord.
If you allow your past mistakes, whatever they
may be, to dominate your present, they will
destroy you. Remember, Dane, we all make
mistakes. God knows that. He forgives us. So
why can't you forgive yourself?"

Samuel left Dane alone to his thoughts as the
shadows of night lengthened and darkness
cloaked the garden. He needed to get home.
But what could he say to Zoey? He had no
answers, but he did have much to think about.

Dane sat at the desk in the den, scribbling his
thoughts in his journal. The second he had
reached home, he had come into the room and
begun writing, reflecting on what Samuel had
said. He'd never written his feelings down
about Jacob's death. He'd always felt if he'd put
them down on paper they would be forever
engraved into his heart. He'd spent so much
time running away from what had happened to
his little brother. It was time he faced it and tried
to deal with it.

His hand trembled as he penned the account

of what had led him to become a DEA agent. As if it were yesterday, he remembered how Jacob had hero-worshipped him, following him around like a lost puppy, looking to him to protect him from the harsh reality of living with their father. But most of all he recalled the night he had discovered Jacob dead from an overdose. That day he had realized he had totally let his little brother down. He'd been too wrapped up in his own life to see that Jacob had turned to something else to help him cope. The memory, that always produced the guilt, tore through him as though a hurricane ravaged him, leaving his soul tattered.

"Dane."

He quickly closed his journal, twisting about to face Zoey. His hands still shaking, he clasped them. "Yes?" was all he managed to say, glad that he had been able to do that much.

"You need to talk to Blake. He needs to hear from you that you are returning home this weekend, that you aren't leaving again, this time for good."

At that moment he wasn't sure he could reassure his son anything. He bled from his shredded emotions. *Where are You, God?* "He should know I'm coming back. I told him."

"You did the last time, too. That's all he remembers."

The rapid thumping of his heart made it difficult even to draw in a decent breath. He nodded and stood, his legs unsteady. He gripped the desk. *God, I need You.*

He plodded past Zoey and up the stairs. He paused; the hallway to Blake's room seemed a mile long. *I don't want to lose my son. Lord, how do I convince him I'm coming home?*

Dane took the first step toward Blake's room. *You aren't alone. I'm with you.*

The comforting words flittered across his mind. His stride lengthened, and before he knew it, he was in front of his son's door. As he raised a hand to knock, a peaceful calm flowed through him.

Dane rapped on the wood once before entering Blake's room.

His son lay on his bed, his arms crossed behind his head. He stared at the ceiling, not saying a word. Suddenly it felt as if he and his son were back to the way it was when he had first returned home.

*You aren't alone.*

Latching on to the serenity he'd experienced in the hallway, Dane crossed the room and sat on the bed.

* * *

The silence of the den taunted Zoey as she paced, waiting for Dane to return. She didn't know how much more of being shut out of his life she could take. Maybe he needed to stay in Dallas. Maybe they needed time and space away from each other. Certainly being in the same house hadn't resolved their problems. In fact, the pain of having him so near and not being an important part of his life hurt her to the point she was beginning to think she might be better off separated from him. She'd managed before. She would again.

The book he had closed when she had come into the den caught her attention. Near the desk she stopped and ran her finger over its black leather. Not really a book. Curious, she opened it, immediately glimpsing Dane's handwriting. The name Jacob in bold black letters leaped off the page. His brother. Quickly she slammed it shut. A journal? Dane?

She took it in her grasp and moved to the couch. Were his thoughts and feelings that he'd kept hidden from her revealed in these pages? Would she finally know what made her husband tick if she read it? She lay the leather-bound journal in her lap, touching its edge with trembling fingers.

Temptation, as she'd never known, over-whelmed her. If only she understood Dane, then maybe there was a chance. All she had to do was open the book and read.

"Blake, let's talk."

His son rolled over onto his side, facing away from him. "There's nothing to talk about."

"Yes, there is. Me leaving."

"What's new?"

"Do you want to come with me?"

Blake twisted around, his eyes round. "You mean it? Come with you to work?"

"I mean it." The second he'd asked his son he'd known this was the right thing to do. No words would reassure Blake totally. Only being with Dane and coming home with him would make his son realize he wasn't going to leave him again.

"What about school?"

"You can miss a few days. I can show you what I do." He also realized he'd never shown Blake what he'd done for a living. His job in his son's mind was mysterious, full of danger, because all he could go on was what he'd seen on television or in the movies. "I'll have to warn you it won't be very exciting."

"This will be so cool. Sean and Craig will be

envious." His huge grin suddenly vanished. "Mom won't let me skip school. She's always said attendance is important."

"Let me handle your mom. Besides, you aren't exactly skipping school. You can take your books with you and work when I'm in meetings."

Blake leaped from the bed and went to his dresser. "I'd better start packing since you're leaving early tomorrow morning."

"Do you have a bag?"

"Yep." Blake opened his closet door and pulled a piece of luggage out.

Dane rose. "Then I'll leave you to pack while I go square this with your mom."

When Dane stepped out into the hallway and was about to close the door, Blake said, "Thanks, Dad. This means a lot to me."

As Dane made his way down the stairs, a lightness took hold of him. Why hadn't he thought to take Blake to work before now? This felt so right and now all he had to do was convince Zoey.

He searched the first floor, puzzled when he didn't find her in the living room or kitchen. Finally he went back to the den where he'd left her earlier and came to an abrupt halt when he found her sitting on the couch with his journal in her lap, her head down, her fingers clasping its edge as though she had just slammed it shut. Anger at her nerve to go through something so private, so personal, chased away all light feelings.

He clenched his hands. "I can't believe what I'm seeing."

She yanked her head up. "I didn't read it. At least not much. I mean, only a word or two."

He strode to her and snatched it from her grasp. "If I had wanted you to read my journal, I would have given it to you. You invaded my privacy."

His words, laced with steel, lashed out at her, cutting through her already fragile emotions. Her own anger burst forth. "Maybe if you shared your feelings with me, I wouldn't have to resort to other means."

She wasn't going to tell him all she had read was his brother's name and the word "was." She'd had it with Dane and his secrets. She'd sat for the past fifteen minutes debating whether to read the journal or not and had finally decided if Dane didn't tell her himself it didn't mean anything to her. If he didn't willingly share his past with her, what good would it do her to find out what he was thinking by going behind his back? The bottom line would be that she would still be excluded from his innermost thoughts.

Dane opened a drawer and tossed the journal inside, then slammed it close. "I'm taking Blake with me to Dallas." He pivoted toward her, his hands curling, then uncurling again into fists.

He was prepared for a battle. She didn't have the energy to fight him anymore. She struggled to her feet, so tired, her hope of making her marriage work gone. She trudged toward the door, needing to leave before she said something she would regret.

But at the entrance she couldn't help but turn and say, "You have shut me out one too many times. I don't see how we can stay together. When you come back, we need to make some hard decisions about our future."

Dane stiffened, his anger disappearing as Zoey did down the hallway. The hurt reflected in her expression stabbed at him. Had he over-reacted to Zoey seeing his journal? He'd never exposed his feelings so much as he had in that book. Throughout his childhood he'd been taught over and over not to share his thoughts. The time he had told his teacher about his dad's drinking he'd been beaten by his father in one of his drunken rages. And worse, no help had arrived on his doorstep because his family had been one of the important ones in the community. All the money in the world hadn't changed what he and his brother had lived through.

After that encounter he had never said anything to anyone about what went on with him. He'd learned to turn inward. He'd learned to hide himself and his brother when his father had started drinking. He'd become quite an expert at that.

And yet, he had demanded Eddy open up to him.

Dane didn't bother setting up the sleeper sofa. Instead he lay down on the couch and stared at the ceiling. With the lights off but the curtains still open, the moon rays danced across the ceiling as clouds drifted across the orb. Exhaustion forced his eyelids closed even though he didn't want to sleep....

*His partner aimed his gun at Dane's heart. The man's betrayal, paid for by the drug lord they had been after, enraged Dane beyond rational thought. When his partner glanced at the pilot to tell him where to go, Dane leaped forward without thought of the consequences. He knocked the gun to the side as Bob squeezed the trigger. The bullet struck the pilot in the back of the head. The man collapsed forward, sending the plane into a nosedive. As the plane headed for the jungle below, Dane struggled with Bob for the weapon....*

Dane's eyes bolted open, sweat drenching him. He remembered everything surrounding his last assignment, especially Bob's defection to the other side. He'd worked with the man for several years and had never suspected until Bob had forced Dane onto the plane. Instead of returning home they were heading to the drug lord's compound in the heart of the jungle. According to Bob, Dane regrettably had become too much of a problem. Bob had been paid handsomely to deliver him to his boss.

Dane pushed to his elbows and looked around the den. Dawn peeked through the open curtains. To think, he had felt guilty for being the only one to survive the plane crash. Yes, he had caused the crash, but it had been him or them. Somehow he had managed to knock Bob out with the butt of the gun, but the plane was too close to the canopy of green for him to do anything about stopping it from crashing. Thinking quickly, he'd opened the door and jumped right before the plane collided with the jungle. He'd hit the top branches of a tree, held on for a few seconds, then plunged to the ground, its hard impact whooshing the breath from him as pain sliced up his legs. He'd crumbled to the ground. The sound of the crash had reverberated through the rain forest as he'd blacked out.

Mopping the sweat from his brow with the edge of his crumpled shirt, Dane swung his legs to the floor. He quaked with the memories flooding his mind.

Slowly he rose. The last piece had fallen into place and with it the knowledge he had messed up his life. He hung his head.

*Lord, Samuel and Zoey have told me You listen when someone is in trouble. I am. I've made such a mess of my life. I don't know what to do to make it right. Is it possible for You to forgive me my mistakes? I've made so many, starting with my little brother and ending with Zoey. I thought if I ran fast enough the past would stay buried. It doesn't. It waits and sneaks up on you when you least expect it. I need You, Lord. Help me.*

# Chapter Thirteen

Mandy's giggle sounded in the silence. Zoey watched her daughter pour tea for Tara, then for Mrs. Giggles and Pepper, and wished life were that simple. Dane had been gone two days, and she still didn't know what to do when he came back. Their marriage wasn't working. She needed a partnership. She needed to feel as important in her husband's life as he was in hers.

These past weeks with him at home had given her a glimpse into what could be. But once Dane let his work absorb him again, she wouldn't see him much. Although she had learned to live her life without him for almost three years, she wanted her husband by her side sharing in his good as well as his bad times. But how could she when he didn't let her in?

"Hi, honey."

Her mother came out onto the deck and took the lounge chair next to hers. Zoey gave her mom a smile she couldn't maintain.

"Aren't Dane and Blake coming home Saturday?"

Zoey nodded, her throat thick with tears that in the past two days had been so close to the surface. She didn't want to admit she'd failed in her marriage, but she didn't know what else to do. She wasn't what Dane wanted or needed. He'd made that plain by shutting her out of his life to the point he would rather put his feelings down in a journal than talk to her.

"Well, then why the long face?"

"Frankly, Mom, I'm not even sure if Dane will stay after he brings Blake back." Staring down, Zoey twisted her hands together in her lap. "We had a terrible fight the night before he went to Dallas. When I took him and Blake to the airport on Wednesday, we hardly said two words to each other. The kids did all the talking." The memory of the silence between them only strengthened her conviction she wasn't what Dane needed.

"What did you two fight about?"

"He thought I read his journal. When I realized that was what it was, I didn't. But I was really tempted to." She lifted her gaze to her mother's, replaying the debate she'd had with herself that night. Her fingers had itched with the desire to open the journal. "I don't know what Dane really feels. There's something in his past eating at him and he won't share it with me. He doesn't trust our love enough to. That hurts so much, Mom."

"Oh, baby, I'm sorry. When your father used to clam up, I would get so mad. But you know I would take his silence for another day with him anytime. Some people, particularly men, don't know how to express their emotions. They have been taught to keep them inside. That doesn't mean he doesn't love you, but he shows his love in a different way."

"To me, trust and love go hand in hand." Zoey thought of the pain that had impaled her heart as she'd watched the plane take off for Dallas. In her mind it had become a symbol of so much of their time together, with her standing by, while her husband left.

"Dane hasn't been back that long. Have you given him enough time to adjust to all the changes that have occurred in your life, in his life?"

"Changes," Zoey murmured, thinking back to the past few years and the necessary adjustments she'd been forced to make when left without a husband.

"You aren't even living in the same town as before. Nothing of his old life is the same. Have you walked in his shoes? How would you feel surrounded with nothing familiar? With pieces of your memory missing?"

Remorse gripped Zoey. No, she hadn't. She'd only looked at the problem from her side. What would it be like to have your life erased then slowly returned bit by bit but not in its entirety? "Mom, I'm not even sure if Dane really loves me."

"Have you asked him? Have you talked to him about this?"

"No, I'm afraid of the answer."

"Why? You sound like you're ready to walk away from your marriage. Don't you think you owe it to him and the children to discover if your love is still alive? Do you love Dane?"

She thought for a long moment, trying to put her swirling emotions concerning Dane into words. In spite of everything that had transpired between them, she couldn't deny her love for Dane. "Yes, I don't think that will ever change. Whether he realizes it or not, he needs me, someone to love and care for him."

"Then, honey, fight for his love."

"How?"

"Pray for guidance. You'll figure something out."

"Dad, your job is so cool."

Dane scribbled his name across his final report concerning the operation in South America. He looked up and grinned at his son.

"Can I come to work with you some other time?"

"We'll see," Dane answered, slipping the paper into the folder.

He wasn't sure where his job would be. Before him was the last sheet he needed to sign—his resignation from the DEA. Coming back to Dallas had only cemented in his mind it was time for him to move on. His heart wasn't in the job like it used to be. He wanted something different from his life. He wanted time to spend with his family, his wife, and if he worked for the agency, he would fall back into the same old pattern—gone all the time, so absorbed in his work that he neglected the people around him. And most of all, he wouldn't give his family what they needed.

"Before we leave, can I watch you shoot again? I can't believe how good you are!"

"Personally I wish I could do my job without the use of a gun. They breed violence." Flashes of the violence in Dane's life flickered across his mind. This fight wasn't his anymore. He wanted peace; he wanted to help in another way. But how?

His boss stuck his head in the doorway. "Have you decided what you want to do? We're finalizing some plans against Juan Sanchez. I think we've finally got him and knew you would want to be in on it."

Dane saw his son's eyes grow round, his body tense, his hands clutched the arms of the chair he sat in. Juan Sanchez was the drug lord he had been after three years ago. He'd always been able to slip through their fingers, and even after Dane's disappearance, the man had managed to—until now. The temptation to be in the thick of things dangled before him like a chocolate cake to a person who'd been fasting for days.

Blake's lips pressed tightly together, his gaze fastened on Dane. His son never released his grip on the arms of the chair.

"Carl, I just signed my resignation right before you came in here."

"We can always tear it up. It's just a piece of paper. Your recovery has been amazing. You've checked out in all areas. We've missed your drive." Carl moved farther into the office. "You don't have to be here in Dallas. You can transfer to our Louisville or Lexington office and still be in on bringing Juan Sanchez down."

The single cake became two. For a few seconds Dane contemplated crumpling up his resignation and continuing doing what he knew how to do best, what he was trained to do. The unknown lay ahead of him. He didn't have a job. He had a family to support. Yes, he had been offered two jobs in Sweetwater. But how good would he be as a police officer or as a youth counselor?

"Dad, aren't we gonna go home tomorrow?"

Blake's question sliced into Dane's thoughts. He focused on Carl, who stood a few feet from him waiting for an answer. "I'm getting out. It's time I left the DEA."

"Frankly I never thought you, of all my agents, would leave."

"I've lost my edge." Dane retrieved the resignation from the desk and handed it to Carl. When his boss took the paper, a peace, like in the hallway of his house a few days before, fell over Dane. It was the right thing to do. The past had controlled his life long enough. Now all he had to do was find a job and convince his wife their marriage could work, that he needed her now more than ever.

As Carl left Dane's office, he thought of the last time he'd seen Zoey at the airport when she'd dropped him and Blake off. She'd kissed her son goodbye and hadn't said a word to him, hadn't even looked at him the whole trip to the airport. Was it too late for them? And if it wasn't, what did he need to do to get her back? He knew the answer the second he thought the question. But he didn't know if he could do what needed to be done.

*Lord, I'm asking for Your help again. Please show me the way.*

"Mom, what are you doing here?" Zoey asked, stepping back to allow her mother into the house.

"Dane called me and asked me if I would come over and babysit while he took you out."

Surprised that Dane had done that having only been home half an hour, Zoey quietly closed the front door. What was her husband up to? On the drive from the airport, they had only shared polite conversation, with the children in the car listening to everything said. Tension still vibrated between them, making Zoey wonder if Dane's offer to take her out was to get her away from the house so he could break the news he had decided to continue his work with the DEA in Dallas.

Zoey heard Dane's footsteps coming down the hall and turned toward her husband. "What's this about going out?"

"I thought we could go for a walk. I'd like to see what they've done with the youth center."

"The youth center? They just started it a few days ago."

"I know. But I feel it's my baby."

Still puzzled by the invitation, Zoey glanced at her mother. "We won't be gone long."

Emma looked behind Zoey toward Dane. "Don't hurry back on my account. I promised Tara and Mandy I would have tea with them. I know it's near dinnertime so I thought we could have a picnic out in the backyard, especially since Blake went over to Sean's. Why don't you two walk into town and grab something at Alice's Café after you see the youth center?"

Dane came to Zoey's side. "We will, Emma. Thanks."

He held the door open for Zoey. Peering at her casual attire of tan slacks and a red blouse, she decided she was dressed all right to go for a walk then to Alice's Café. Out on the porch

Dane didn't pause but kept going down the steps. At the bottom he finally turned and waited for her. When she came abreast of him, he took her hand and started down the street toward the church and youth center.

The late afternoon was beautiful with a light breeze stirring the trees and cooling the warm air. A hint of a sweet flower wafted to Zoey. She scanned the area and decided it was the climbing red roses along Wilbur's white picket fence.

The sedate pace and silence eroded Zoey's composure. If she had to move back to Dallas, she wanted to know now so she could start preparing herself. For the past twenty-four hours she had prayed over what she should do and had come to the decision the family needed to stay together even if it meant going back to Dallas.

The light feel of Dane's hand around hers gave her the confidence to say, "I realized it was wrong of me to tell you I wouldn't move back to Dallas if you went back to your old job." The very thought of leaving Sweetwater broke her heart, but the chance to repair her marriage was more important. "I don't want to live there, but I still think we need to stay together for the kids' sake."

"Only for them?"

He kept walking while Zoey halted in the middle of the street. "We have to consider the children."

He pivoted a few feet in front of her and faced her with a neutral look that slowly evolved into a grin, his eyes twinkling. "I was thinking we should stay together for *our* sake. After all, what will we do when Tara leaves home in, say, sixteen years? Then it will be just you and me."

Zoey placed a hand on her waist. "What's going on, Dane? Are you staying in Dallas? Are you working for the DEA?"

The breeze picked up slightly, teasing a strand of his hair. He plowed his fingers through it to brush the stray lock out of his face. "I have to say, Zoey, I'm mighty touched that you would even consider going back to Dallas to keep our family together. But I have to disappoint you. I've resigned from the DEA."

Stunned, Zoey let her arm fall to her side. Then pure elation zipped through her, and she threw herself into Dane's embrace, kissing him on the mouth. "You did! That's great!"

He laughed. "I take it you don't mind having an unemployed husband then?"

"That won't last long at all." She snuggled against his chest, feeling his heart pounding beneath her palm, its fast tempo matching the pace of hers.

"Actually it may only last a day or so."

She pulled back and stared into his eyes. "What are you thinking of doing? Taking Zach up on the offer to be on the Sweetwater police force?"

"I called Samuel last night and told him I'd be the head of the youth center if he still wanted me."

Zoey's lower jaw dropped. Dane put a finger under her chin and pushed up gently.

"You're going to be a counseler?"

He nodded slowly, his mouth twisting into a wry grin. "I may be rusty. I might have to get pointers from you."

"But I thought you didn't—"

He pressed his finger to her lips to still her words. "Let's not continue this conversation until we can have some privacy. I've got just the place. I've got things I want to tell you."

Taking her hand again, he tugged her to his side and slipped his arm around her, then set out toward the church. She thought of how perfect she fit against him. He strolled to the center of the Garden of Serenity by the fish pond and settled himself next to her on a bench.

Above them a mockingbird trilled a beautiful song while perched on the branch of the dogwood tree, its white flowers gone now that it was nearing summer. The sound of the water trickling across the rocks competed with the bird to fill the silence between her and Dane. She waited for him to begin, her breath captured in her lungs.

He inhaled deeply, then released it slowly. "I'm not very good at pouring my heart out. I hope practice makes perfect."

A few seconds passed, and Zoey started to say something when Dane continued. "You're aware that I had a little brother who died young, but I never shared with you how. In fact, I did my best to try and forget how. I think it's about time I tell you since it's the driving reason behind so much of what I've done."

Dane searched for her hand resting between them on the bench and clasped it. Again he pulled a gulp of air into his lungs. "This isn't easy for me, Zoey, but you need to know it."

"Take your time. Mom's got the kids."

He squeezed her hand and brought it up to lay in his lap, cupping it between both of his. "I tried to protect Jacob the best I could from our dad. Most of the time I was successful, but occasionally Dad got ahold of him when he had been drinking and slapped him around. I was twelve when our mom died. That's when Dad began to drink all the time. Before that, not too often. She seemed to have a calming effect on our dad that I never did."

"That should never be a child's job, Dane." She'd seen this before in students she had counseled and it was never easy—the child becoming the parent.

"I know that in my mind but—" he brought their linked hands up so he could touch the place over his heart "—not in here. Whenever I couldn't protect my little brother, I felt I had let him down somehow. I should have been able to protect him."

"Did you have anyone you could tell?"

"I tried once to let my aunt know but she wouldn't listen. Also, a teacher, but my dad had some influence in the town and people didn't believe me. By the time I turned sixteen, Dad didn't threaten Jacob or me any longer. I was bigger than my father by then. That's why I didn't go away to college. I needed to be there for Jacob.

"When our father died, I began to look after Jacob since I was twenty. Jacob was fifteen at the time."

When Dane paused, his eyes sliding close, Zoey turned toward him, wanting to get as close to him as possible. "I'm so sorry about your father. No wonder Eddy's plight got to you."

"By the time Jacob was sixteen he was into drugs, but I didn't know it. I was too wrapped up into going to college to be a counselor so I could help others who had gone through a similar situation like me. I was also working thirty-five hours a week so I could keep Jacob with me. By the time my father died, the family's money was almost completely gone." He paused for a few seconds, staring up into the tree above him. "I failed my little brother. The signs were there. I just didn't want to see them. Where Jacob was concerned I had blinders on."

"We never want to believe the worst of our loved ones."

"He was crying out for help, and I wasn't listening. He finally took an overdose and died on my bed when I was at the clinic at school running a counseling session. I was late getting home that night or I might have been there in time. Sometimes I wonder if he had really wanted to do it or was just trying to get my attention and it went too far. I'll never know, but it has eaten at me for years. If I hadn't stayed that extra half hour, I could…"

Zoey's breath caught, the picture that popped

into her mind sending a shudder through her. "Oh, Dane," she murmured, her throat clogged with tears. Guilt drove people to do so many things.

"I tried to revive Jacob while I waited for the ambulance. He never regained consciousness. After that I changed my focus. I wasn't going to let others go through what I did. I was in my last year of college and decided to use my psychology training to catch the people who prey on other's weaknesses."

The tremor in his voice misted her eyes. A lone tear slipped down her cheek.

"As you know, right out of college I joined the DEA and you know the rest. My life became a crusade against any person selling or manufacturing drugs. I was determined to rid the world of every drug dealer there was." His body shook with his journey into the past. He slanted a pained look toward her. "Naive, wasn't it?"

"If there weren't people like you trying, the drug problem would be worse than it is."

"After Jacob's death I didn't think I could counsel anyone. How could I when I let my own brother down? I tried once at the halfway house and failed miserably."

"Is that why you refused Samuel's suggestion to run the youth center?"

Dane nodded, visibly swallowing as he stared off into the distance. "Then Eddy came along and showed me there was a need in Sweetwater. Blake's problems only confirmed the necessity for me to be around more than I have been. I haven't been here for you or the children much, even before my disappearance. That's gonna change now." He slid a half grin toward her. "You all might get tired of me after a few months."

"I think we'll manage."

He took her into his arms. "I won't be an open book, but I'll try to share my feelings more. Writing in that journal has helped. The psychologist I saw when I first came back from the Amazon suggested I do that. It was awkward at first, but now I actually look forward to it. I even think the journal has made telling you easier." Cradling her head, he peered into her gaze. "I love you, Zoey. That's an emotion I'm one hundred percent sure of."

Tears of joy flooded her eyes. "I love you. That's why everything hurt so much."

"Your decision to move back to Sweetwater was a good one. When I was in Dallas at the office, all I could think about was something to do with this town. I haven't been here two months and it's already in my blood."

"Sweetwater has a way of doing that to a person. Then you really don't mind staying in a small town and not working at the DEA?"

"When I signed my resignation, I experienced a peace I never have before. Helping kids work through their problems is what I should do. I wasn't there for Jacob, but maybe I can be for someone else. I can't bring my little brother back, but I might be able to stop some other kid from going down that path. I'm certainly going to try."

Zoey wound her arms around his neck, compelling him to look at her. "You did the best you could. You're looking at the situation through hindsight. We can always see our mistakes then. You took your brother in, you provided for him and protected him as much as you could. Sometimes what we do isn't always enough, but that doesn't mean we spend the rest of our lives beating ourselves up over it."

"I know that now. I figured if God can forgive me, I can forgive myself. Eddy has shown me a path I had forsaken in my grief and it feels right."

Zoey tugged Dane's head down, pressing his lips into hers. As his kiss deepened, he brought her up on his lap and cuddled her against him, the racing of his heart matching hers.

# *Epilogue*

"Where in the world did you get these huge scissors?" Dane asked, taking the pair from Zoey.

"It wasn't easy. But I wanted something special for this ribbon-cutting ceremony. It isn't everyday my husband gets to open a youth center he's going to run." Zoey faded back into the line of people crowded around the entrance into the Sweetwater Youth Center.

Dane stood next to Samuel in front of the red ribbon slung across the double doors into the two-story building. He held the oversized scissors in position as Samuel quieted the throng of well-wishers.

"It's been four months since Dane Wither-spoon suggested this center for the youth in Sweetwater. A place for them to hang out after school and during the holidays. A place where they can come for help and guidance. A safe haven. Probably sometime in the future we would have finally gotten around to proposing the youth center, but it took this man beside me to prod us into doing it, not just talking about it. And the best part is he has agreed to run the center for us. His background in counseling made him an excellent candidate for the position, but mostly it is his caring nature that will make him a success. So without further ado, let's go inside and see the new center."

With flushed cheeks, Dane took his cue and snipped the ribbon, then stepped forward to open the doors for the crowd to enter. He stood on one side while Samuel was on the other, greeting everyone as they went into the building.

Zoey hung back and watched her husband shake hands with the people filing into the center. Her chest swelled with pride at how much Dane had come to fit into Sweetwater, as though he had grown up in the town. He'd even wooed Wilbur to his way of thinking.

Beth came to her side and leaned close. "You all coming to dinner tonight?"

"Of course. Anytime I don't have to cook is great."

"Good, because I had one of my nights where I cooked for hours and have way too much food. I've got to get rid of it."

Zoey slanted a look at her friend. "What's got you worried?"

"Craig and Blake's band are playing this afternoon at the grand opening of the center. He doesn't seem to get nervous whenever he plays, but I do enough worrying for every boy in the band."

"They've done great at church. They've been practicing a lot lately. They'll do fine."

"That's what Samuel and Dane keep telling me, but a mother's job is to worry."

Zoey noticed the crowd thinning out and started to move toward Dane. "Worrying will only give you gray hairs."

"I'm still new at this mothering role. I wish I could be as laid-back as you."

The sound of a popular song drifted to Zoey. "They've started. Let's get inside. I don't want to miss any of their performance."

Samuel and Beth walked into the building ahead of them. Dane pulled Zoey against his side and slipped his arm around her shoulders. The chords on the keyboard Blake played filled the air with harmony while the sun shone down and the smells of summer laced the breeze.

"Thank you, Zoey Witherspoon, for making these past months the best ones I've ever had. I didn't think it was possible for my love to grow but it has."

Zoey stared into his dark gaze and realized all her dreams had come true. She had a family and a loving, caring husband, an equal partner who gave of himself.

\* \* \* \* \*

*Look for Tanya's story,*
*TIDINGS OF JOY, out in October,*
*only from Margaret Daley*
*and Love Inspired.*

Dear Reader,

This story about Zoey and Dane is about love, hope and second chances. Their faith was tested in *When Dreams Come True*. When life intruded, separating them, Zoey turned to the Lord and her faith to get her through the ordeal. Dane turned away, floundering on his own. Often in life we are given second chances. Sometimes we fail to make them work. Sometimes we are lucky enough to grasp them and reclaim what is precious. Dane had to learn to put trust in the Lord, himself and Zoey. He also had forgotten how to let go of the past and trust again. Trust is at the heart of most successful relationships, whether with the Lord or a loved one.

Another issue I dealt with in this story was learning when to get help. Eddy had trouble dealing with his situation concerning his father's drinking. It is important for people dealing with a loved one who is an alcoholic to get help. There are organizations to help. One of them is Al-Anon. You can get information at www.al-anon.alateen.org.

I love hearing from readers. You can contact me at P.O. Box 2074, Tulsa, OK 74101, or visit my Web site at www.margaretdaley.com.

Best wishes,

*Margaret Daley*

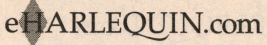

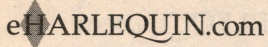

# eHARLEQUIN.com

## The Ultimate Destination for Women's Fiction

### Visit eHarlequin.com's Bookstore today for today's most popular books at great prices.

- An extensive selection of romance books by top authors!
- Choose our convenient "bill me" option. No credit card required.
- New releases, Themed Collections and hard-to-find backlist.
- A sneak peek at upcoming books.
- Check out book excerpts, book summaries and Reader Recommendations from other members and post your own too.
- Find out what everybody's reading in Bestsellers.
- Save BIG with everyday discounts and exclusive online offers!
- Our Category Legend will help you select reading that's exactly right for you!
- Visit our Bargain Outlet often for huge savings and special offers!
- Sweepstakes offers. Enter for your chance to win special prizes, autographed books and more.

### Your purchases are 100% guaranteed—so shop online at www.eHarlequin.com today!

# eHARLEQUIN.com

## The Ultimate Destination for Women's Fiction

### Calling all aspiring writers!
Learn to craft the perfect romance novel
with our useful tips and tools:

- Take advantage of our **Romance Novel Critique Service** for detailed advice from romance professionals.

- Use our **message boards** to connect with writers, published authors and editors.

- Enter our **Writing Round Robin**— you could be published online!

- Learn many tools of the writer's trade from editors and authors in our **On Writing** section!

- **Writing guidelines** for Harlequin or Silhouette novels—what our editors *really* look for.

**Learn more about romance writing
from the experts—
visit www.eHarlequin.com today!**